Ngahuia Te Awekotuku was born and grew up in Ohinemutu, Rotorua, where most of these stories are set. She has a long involvement in Maori, gay, and women's issues, especially in Auckland and Hamilton. She now lectures in art history at Auckland University, and is contributing to the planning of the new national arts centre in Wellington.

Other titles in the
International Connections Series:

The Shrunken Dream
by Jane Tapsubei Creider

Tahuri

Short Stories By

Ngahuia Te Awekotuku

CANADIAN CATALOGUING IN PUBLICATION DATA
Te Awekotuku, Ngahuia
Tahuri : short stories
(International connections : women writers from around the world)
North American ed.
ISBN 0-88961-183-1
1. Women — Maori — New Zealand — Fiction.
2. Lesbians — Fiction. I. Title. II. Series.

PR9639.3.T42T34   1993   823   C93-093391-5

Copyright © 1993 Ngahuia Te Awekotuku
Cover illustration: Kathryn Madill
Cover design: Sunday Harrison
Series design: Denise Maxwell
Originally published by New Women's Press, New Zealand
(1989 and 1991), this North American edition is published by
Women's Press, #233-517 College Street,
Toronto, Ontario, Canada, M6G 4A2.
Available outside North America from New Women's Press.

All rights reserved. No part of this book may be used or reproduced in any manner whatsoever without written permission except in the case of brief quotations embodied in critical articles and reviews. For information contact Women's Press (Canada) at the above address.

This book was produced by the collective effort of Women's Press. Women's Press gratefully acknowledges the financial support of the Canada Council and the Ontario Arts Council.

1 2 3 4 5   1997 1996 1995 1994 1993

Contents

Auntie Marleen   9

The Basketball Girls   11

After the Game   16

Three for Kui   19

Uncle Ted in the Big Truck   25

It Looks Pretty Dopey to Me   26

Koura   31

Tahuri: the Runaway   34

Paretipua   53

Old Man Tuna   55

Watching the Big Girls   60

Sunday Drive   65

Rainy Day Afternoon   68

Olympia   72

Mirimiri   76

Red Jersey   95

Words Used in the Text   101

Although I have drawn on my own life for
many of these stories, they are works of fiction.
Any resemblance to anyone, living or
gone, is not intended.

He tohu aroha tenei ki taku kuia
For my Grandmother

Auntie Marleen

They were off in the taxi, Mum and her husband, just as Auntie Marleen came through the door, following her smells, which always came in first. Grease, sour tobacco, and oiled rows of chestnut hair running short-cropped from the forehead to the neck. Motorbike fumes, dust, and worn-out leather in the soft brown folds of her fighter pilot's coat. She was my babysitter; she'd arrive in a crackle of smoke — from her Three Castles roll-your-own and her machine's exhaust – and she'd pull up by the house, the engine of her Norton chugging reluctantly to a standstill. With a smile to my mother, and a slight nod to the man at her side, she marched smartly up the back steps, her heavy lace-up shoes creaking, the sharp grey edges of her flannel trousers catching the sun.

She had a routine, which was always strictly followed. She would shake my hand, and I'd always wonder at the coolness of her ivory white fingers, and severely clipped nails, and the spoiled bit of skin, stained by nicotine. Then she would take off her coat and unroll a long green knitted scarf from around her neck, revealing a buttoned shirt collar sitting above a thick navy blue pullover. The shirt was blue, too. She'd hang the coat and scarf on the back door hook, taking some stuff out of the pockets. Three Castles, matches in a Beehive box, blackballs, and a book, red cloth covered with brittle library plastic. The Famous Five again. I watched, thinking greedily about a blackball, melting sweet and gooey in my mouth, as she made two cups of cocoa. And with the Famous Five's latest adventure tucked into her armpit, the drinks steaming and balanced in one hand, and the blackballs in the other, she walked ahead of me, into the bedroom.

After the cocoa, I was allowed one blackball. Just one, which I'd clatter between my teeth and lick beneath my tongue, willing it to last and last. And as she turned the fourth page, my head heavy with the cocoa, and the day's activities, I was out cold . . .

Auntie Marleen's voice was like that – soft and low and droning, even at the most exciting bits, where Jo catches the runaway horse, or Quentin grabs the smuggler; Auntie Marleen's quiet monotone stayed on the same dogged, slow, dreary level, and I drifted quietly away, safe in the murmur of the story . . .

That was part of the routine too; that I fell asleep early, so that she would go back to the kitchen, make another cup of cocoa, turn on the wireless, and read the paper. She was doing this one night when I had to go to the lav; she didn't notice me creeping around; she was behind the paper hidden by clouds of curling tobacco smoke.

Auntie Marleen. She had broken little teeth with mossy brown edges from all the smoking; and an awkward, rare lopsided smile, so that if she smiled, she showed only the left side of her jaw – where the teeth were not so bad. Her skin was downy and sallow, and moved a lot as she talked; soft creases and deep grooves around her very neat, very straight nose. And her eyes were kind and hollow, the colour of fading autumn leaves; sad. She never ever laughed.

Auntie Marleen gave me my first cat.

And my very first look at what I could become.

The Basketball Girls

Tihi looked at herself in the mirror. Closely, critically. Decided she was ready to go out into the kitchen and show herself off to the family – Koro and the kids, maybe an auntie or two or three, having a cup of tea and warming their feet by the coal range.

Everyone – everything – stopped as she came through the door. Tall, fair, and slim. She let them all inspect her; she was proud of her long shapely legs in the sheer black stockings (two and eleven from Matthias, what a bargain eh), her firm supple knees (she was too quick to fall, and much too vain to graze them on the knotty asphalt court); and her flexibly fine ankles cased in the black canvas boots. Tihi was a Basketball Girl. And she was one of the best.

And oh, how I loved to look at her. Saturday afternoons that winter, off I'd rush next door, straight after breakfast, quick as whitebait, into Koro's kitchen to ogle and admire. Staring at Tihi was a treat. And following her from a safe distance was even more of a treat, as long as we didn't 'cramp my style, you kids'.

She'd meet her mates at the Hindu shop. Two of them, Cindy and Pera. And they'd buy soft drinks in slender glass bottles, with long wax pink straws. Green River, they'd say. Matching the colour of our girdles and ties. Green River – for luck.

Meanwhile, we'd all be hanging back – if there was a gang of us – and we'd wait for the bottles, which were dropped more or less in the same place every time. One with a chewed straw (Pera), one with the straw rammed and buckled in the bottle (Cindy), and one still neat and whole (Tihi). Each bottle was worth fourpence. Three made a shilling. Wow, that was a fortune!

Which I never made, for I was too busy watching Tihi. She walked like a princess. Very straight, yet there was a ripple in there too. Maybe like a panther, with her long black legs. Her gym was always pressed and almost sharp at the edges of every one of her six box pleats – three in front, and three at the back, that made twelve edges. Done early every Saturday morning, with the iron hot from the range, and a well-scrubbed, damp, worn-out flour bag with the edges picked out. Every pleat was just right; so that the gym hung from her shoulders like a straight black box, with big sections in it, like panels. Over a snowy white long-sleeved blouse, with a specially stiffened collar. And a carefully knotted emerald green tie. Koro himself taught Tihi how to do the tie up 'tika' – properly; and he was truly pleased with himself that day, folding the green silk fabric in his barky old fingers, chuckling at his attentive mokopuna. Tihi. Te Tihi Teitei o Kahukura. The highest arch of Kahukura; Rainbow's End. She was well named. And she showed how well she'd learned to do the tie, by skilfully knotting the girdle as well. The colour of new spring grass, woven into a length of narrow wool, two yards long, cutting the box pleats in half, nipping into her waist, lifting the hem even shorter! This always interested me – the gym no longer looked like a big black box; it pulled out very slightly over Tihi's chest, while still going straight down the back, though all the pleats gathered and crimped, just a little way over the girdle, and fell in a skirt to the middle of her thighs.

Underneath the hem were other things too; they popped and snapped and kept the black stockings up, pulling taut an inky black line that ran from her heel all the way up the back of her leg. Cindy, Pera, and Tihi spent a lot of time worrying about these lines – those damn seams they were called, as the three twirled and danced and twisted, craning their necks over their shoulders, peering down at the back of their knees. Pera had the most trouble; she was shorter, but somehow much fuller, and though she ironed her gym just like Tihi, it just flared and flounced, swelling out in the front at the top, and jutting like a shelf from the back of her bum. So her hem was sort of even.

Tihi always made sure her damn seams were straight. 'Cos that's a *rule*', Pera would roll the words out, husky and rich, and they'd laugh and laugh. Even Cindy, who seemed a bit sour, she'd laugh in a gravelly, raw-voiced way. Her knees were always grazed, her eyes were always there, on Tihi. They would shine like dark embers from her strong face; though not the prettiest, she was the tallest in their trio. And she starred on the basketball court, shot after shot after shot.

Off down the street they'd stride, arms linked. Tihi in the middle, Pera on the right, Cindy on the left, all in rhythm. The Basketball Girls. Pleased with the world, and with each other. Going to meet their mates. Going to play the game. Going to win.

Saturday after Saturday, I followed them, and I wondered at their pride, and their grace, and their beauty. Even on wet days, when the rain lashed the asphalt like acid, and their boots would slide and slip, their pony tails flop and straggle. Even on days when they got 'cleaned up', usually by a visiting team from a bigger town – because at home, they knew they were the best. They had the trophies to prove it. And Auntie Lily, with her green lapels lined with a brazen glitter of badges, she said so. She was the coach, and a ref, and the selector, and she knew. That was that.

So spring came, and all the skinny willow trees turned the colour of the river, and the season was over. No more basketball till next year. No more following Tihi and her mates down the street on a Saturday afternoon. No more till next year.

And eventually, next year, winter, arrived. After a summer of blinding white softball pants and Tihi with a sunburned nose and cracked mouth and peroxide streak in her hair. Which was still in a ponytail, with the same green ribbon.

Winter arrived. And with it came Ahi. In a gleaming two-toned Zephyr Six, with bright red stars that flashed like rubies on the fenders. Ahi turned up to take Tihi to basketball, every Saturday. Just Tihi, because Pera had moved to the coast to look after her Kuia, and Cindy – well, she had just sort of vanished. Dropped out of sight. Who knew where.

Still young, still nosey, I'd hang around next door while Tihi got ready for the game. She still had that magic for me, even though she didn't meet her two mates any more at the Hindu shop; and with no Green River bottles to fight over, the other kids weren't interested in staying around. Tihi would meet Ahi instead; Ahi, who pulled up in the gateway in that amazing car. Ahi, with thick, jet black hair cut like Elvis but a little longer at the back, like a fat duckbum. And dark glasses, green green glass in thick plastic frames. Ahi, who never smiled . . . and never got out of the car to go in and meet Koro either. Just waited, quietly, then revved the motor as Tihi gaily pranced out, flipped open the passenger door, kissed Ahi on the cheek, and then with a filmstar wave at her greatest fan (me) was off. Down the road with Ahi, who somehow felt familiar to me. Somehow.

Then it happened. Koro had a turn one Saturday morning, just as Tihi was ironing the sleeves of her blouse. She rushed out the door and was back in five minutes with Auntie Nel who had a car and worked at the hospital. They took Koro up there, where he was to stay and get fussed over for a couple of weeks.

And I was told to wait, and tell Ahi.

Oh, I thought, my eleven-year-old brain buzzing with the responsibility, my face a smear of tears. What was I going to say?

The car pulled up, all polished and shining. Ahi was checking the dark glasses in the rear-vision mirror. Slowly, I walked over, carefully arranging my story. It still came out all garbled though, but Ahi got the message, while I blubbered on pitifully.

The car door opened, and Ahi got out, kneeled down, still not saying a word. One strong arm went around me. I stopped snivelling, leaned into the black satin shirt of Tihi's hero, Ahi. Who took off the dark glasses, and looked at me. Smiling, talking softly in a voice I *knew*!

'Don't worry, Huri girl, Koro will be fine, you'll see.'

It was Cindy. Ahi had Cindy's eyes, and Cindy's voice. Cindy had come back as Ahi. Wow! It felt like a secret – it felt neat, though! I was dying to run away and tell someone.

But I didn't. I just went to church and to youth club and to school and waited for Saturday mornings. And the magic of Tihi, getting ready for the game, getting ready for Ahi.

Getting ready for us.

After the Game

Hard game, that one. The girls sat by the foot pools at Kuirau, stuffed. All the pleats gone in their coarse hockey shirts, and the heavy socks gored with mud. Why not get right in? Leave our sticks over there. We all got a change, eh girls. Let's warm ourselves up.

Sure thing.

Softness of the healing waiariki - bruises lifting like fabric from the bloodied shins; full breasts and unclipped bras and plump arms floating on the surface of the gentle water - laughter through the steam; dense shimmering curls of light and shadow. So warm, so very very warm.

He oranga mo te tinana. Healthy.

Daylight fading quickly. The skin changing colour.

They relaxed, enjoying the soak, enjoying the big risk they were taking, because the waiariki here was no longer theirs. Not any more - it belonged to the Borough Council, and that was that. If anyone from the Borough Council offices caught them - if a ranger came by, say, or one of those hoity-toity old bags from the front counter where you paid your rates - well, they'd be in for it, then. But that wasn't likely, on a day like this. With the rain belting down on and off, and the hautonga whistling in from the south. Pakehas like that stayed home all cosy and safe on wet Saturdays, and they drank tea and did their knitting and read books.

That's what the girls thought, as they turned their tired ankles in small circles, soothing, and flexed their bumpy knees.

Auntie Pani started telling one of her stories. This one was a beaut, and all her chins waggled with excitement, and her left eye, slightly lopsided, winked wickedly at her niece, closest to her, head just above the surface of the water, ears glowing in the heat, hair slicked about her neck like leaves of long wet grass.

'We were getting into the bus,' she nodded solemnly, 'to go to the hui. And the old lady decided she was coming too, cough and all. Well, you know you can't tell that one anything,' – murmurs of understanding whispered around the pool – 'so it's a good thing I'd packed her Baxters and her blankets just in case, 'cos you never know. There she was, arguing about her seat, that tokotoko going flat out, in the air and all over the place, she was having a great time! She wouldn't get on the bus until Muri had moved. Well. Along comes this tourist, cuts across the front to Tama, over the marae, just like that. Quick as a bloody flash, up comes the camera. Snap! Ko porangi hoki te kuia naana. The old dear went berserk and took to him with her tokotoko – all the taiaha training was right there, and boy, did she give him a few good ones. Ha. He couldn't get away 'cos we all closed in and cut him off, while she let the bugger have it! Bloody good job, too – the old lady hoodoo'd his camera, you know. Photos like that of her never ever come out. Never. In the end we let him go and he ran up the road like a scared rabbit! Did we have a good laugh! The cheeky bastard. Mind you, it perked the kuia up, and she was in top form for the rest of the trip, she was fantastic! He got what he deserved, that pakeha, and so did she – a bit of action for once! She gets so restless these days – there's only half a dozen like her left now, with the moko, and they're so frail and sickly. But her – her – she'll go down fighting, that's for sure.'

'Hey, Bun, we need a new bouncer at the pub,' someone piped up. 'What d'you reckon?' Snorts of grinning approval.

'Sounds all right. But what about her tokotoko? With that, she's armed and dangerous, eighty-one or not! It's a deadly weapon!'

'You ask her then, Bun,' everyone agreed. 'See what the old duck says.' They chuckled quietly.

Bulky shape suddenly there in the gathering dark. They all sat up, alert, silent. Huh. Pakeha with a camera. Big one, too. Levelling it. Like a gun. At the girls.

'If you wanna take a photo of us, then you gotta get permission from our great-grandmother, see. Or else you hop in with us, okay? Strip off. Get in the water. Yep. Right in. Like this.'

'It's the traditional Maori way,' someone else said, not batting an eyelid. 'Otherwise . . .'

Ominous giggles floated from the shadows, from the steam. Sprung, the tourist stepped back. He noticed a pile of long wooden objects on the ground. Weapons? He swiftly returned his camera to his blue Pan Am bag, deciding not to take a photo after all. He turned and walked quickly away.

Husky laughter followed him along the path.

Three for Kui

Cold Night at the Big House

They all seemed to come through the double doors at once – the four aunties, the Big Sisters, chattering and laughing and shivering about the cold. Great heavy coats were flung over chairs, and scarves unwound, gloves removed. Combs were adjusted carefully, and fingernails inspected, too. Frozen feet in woolly socks – dainty feet, though – tramped across the flowery mats, towards the fireplace, where chopped manuka blazed in a reddening iron grate; where the flames danced and flirted, making Tahuri's heart very warm, and her cheeks even warmer still . . .

She sat in a corner, folded up against her Kuia's big round knees. The old lady was dozing, unaware of her noisy chattering nieces; comfortable in the fat green armchair, she had simply drifted away in the fire's glow, her hands twined in her mokopuna's hair, her glasses crooked on her fine brown nose, her mouth ever so slightly open and whistling delicately, softly. Tahuri smiled and snuggled closer, watching the Big Sisters.

The three oldest – and biggest – and bossiest – had ordered Auntie Tia to make a cup of tea, and she was clattering and complaining in the kitchen through the wall. Clunk, clunk, clatter, complain.

Meanwhile, her sisters were jockeying for position in front of the fire. And with a lot of to-ing and fro-ing they were set, after piling two more crackling scented logs of last year's wood, husk dry, into the flames. Waves of heat billowed across the room, and shadows flickered and scampered across the calendar and Queen's picture, and Auntie Tia's teaching certificate in its black frame.

Each one of the three Biggest Sisters gave a sigh – as hearty as her own full-bosomed chest – and relaxed, completely.

Together they hitched up their wide gathered skirts and scooped their petticoats neatly, and with considerable sensitivity and caution, they placed their bloomered bums above the grate. They were set. All lined up.

'Aaaah,' they smiled in unison. 'Nice warm fire. It's so cold outside.'

Request Session

The wallpaper was the fading pink of a pakeha baby's powdered bum, with little floral dimples scattered across it in showers. Tahuri picked at a flower with her hairclip. Pick, pick, pick. She screwed and poked at it until a tiny ragged hole had blossomed on the wall.

Damn, she thought. Now Kuia will get mad at me. She turned over on the narrow bed, pulled the itchy green blankets up to her ears, and peered over her shoulder. Kuia was a quietly snoring hump on the other side of the room, not far away, just an arm-stretch, in fact. Close enough to reach out and touch, just to make sure, on those terrifying, terrible nights when Tahuri woke up and the small room was deathly (yes, deathly!) silent, and Kuia was lying there still, like a stone, still. Motionless. And in her panic, the mokopuna would stretch out her hand and fumble around and pretend to be looking for a sock or something and turn on the light (if things looked really bad) and then with a gush of joyous relief, watch the old lady irritably and inevitably snort herself awake. They were trying times – for Tahuri, the snoring, no matter how thunderous or trumpeting, was a sign of precious life, and silence was *not*.

Kuia was quietly whistling and whirruping and Tahuri smiled, turned the radio on. The Request Session.

'For the girls in Form Five B at Queen Vic from the Tip Boys after a Hui Topu to remember. Kia ora girls and here's your song . . .' about a yellow bird up high in a banana tree.

Yellow bird, yellow bananas. Tahuri drifted.

What were those girls like? Form Five B. They must be Big

Girls, going to a Hui Topu like that, she pondered. A Hui Topu to remember. Yeah.

Next came her hero, the King himself, wanting to be a Teddy Bear, for Janine from Nelson, Pat and Hemi from Kaeo, Teeny and Bob on their engagement with love from Clarissa, two toots from Tutata at Te Kaha, and a special hello to Chrissie, Violet, Orewa and Hine at Rangiatea in New Plymouth. Good on you girls, the announcer chirped. Work hard and pass your Maori test on Monday.

Hey, that's tomorrow, Tahuri thought to herself. Going to school away from home, wonder what that's like? It sounds neat to me, I wish I could. Just being with other Maori girls all day and no fighting on the way to school and no scraps with those kehas. Be neat all right. She turned again, lovingly patted a compact little black furry shape curled tight against her knees. But, Kuia wouldn't be there and I couldn't have you on my bed, eh Sammy...

'Twilight Time' filled the bedroom, shimmering through the worn lace curtains, caught in the soft moonlight. Tahuri fumbled around underneath the bed, looking for her songster – this was one she wanted to learn, get the words off perfect for when she went singing on the river bank with her cousin Donna. She gave up in the dark, the cold too much, and plonked back into her warm bed, listening to the list of names that sounded like a poem – Hineahi, Jason and Materoa from Tolaga, how are you going down there, okay? Jolene and Fergus from Lower Hutt and here's a big bunch all the lads in Four General at Te Aute good on you boys and here's a note from Arthur for Jenny in Lower Hutt and we're playing this for Glenys and Sheena and Marilynn and Keri and Linda and Tawhiri, one for you by the Platters... 'Twilight Time'...

And for Jimbo and Fanny at Kaharoa; Tawhai, Bubbah and Maxie-Boy in Wanganui; all the girls in Three Cee at Hook; the Rhumbah Twins at Pukekohe; Phyllis and Phoebe down town; Mavis, John, Betty and Hika celebrating their anniversaries; for Chacha and Raewyn and their little sister Suzie, yes, it's the sensational Supremes with 'Baby Love'... here they were on the bedroom wall, pinned up and shining, eyes bright and wide and promising, with huge crowns of hair and slinky green dresses and flashing white white teeth ... the Supremes. Kuikui always blinked at them in the morning, said they looked like her nieces, Kara's family ... Tahuri didn't think so; the Supremes were flash ... She rocked and wiggled to the energy of their song, careful not to creak the bedsprings, mouthing the words not quite out loud and stretching her arms in the air, dramatically.

Sammy gave up with a sniffy meow, and rolled herself to the very end of the bed, snuggling up in an old cardigan. She purred. The song finished. Tahuri lay there, almost exhausted. And then she heard it – her own request – wow! Fantastic! She sat up in bed so suddenly, Sammy fell off with a startled squeak. It had worked! It had got to them. Like magic, on the back of the envelope just like they said! Her big show-off big-shot show business cousins singing Kuia's favourite song, requested by Tah-hoo-ree in Sulphur City Roh-toh-rooh-ah-

'Haruru ana te rongo pai e . . .' and she was transfixed.

Her name on the radio, on the request session, just like the girls, the important ones, from Queen Vic and Hook and Rangiatea, just like them!

She swayed with delight to the music. Too soon, it was over. Her Kuia stirred quietly in the next bed; a rumbling and falling of quilts and eiderdown. 'That a good song, Huri,' she sighed, her old voice a caress. 'Kaati now, kare. Turn the radio off now . . .'

Waipuke

Outside the wind had stopped, but she could hear the rain was still coming down in buckets. Tahuri's eyes snapped open. It was Saturday and no school and maybe there was a flood!

She jumped out of bed and pulled her jeans over her jamas and grabbed her old woolly shirt and raincoat. Kui's bed was already made, which meant she'd been up for ages already. Oh well. She tugged on her boots. Flung the front door open and got a shock.

Murky brown water lapped the concrete of the very top step. And there, wading through the hungry howling river that had swallowed up her whole garden, was Kuikui. Head bent against the rain, her skirts gathered up to her hips, her huge gumboots sloshing. Underneath each arm two chickens were clamped firmly to her side and on her back, sewn up screeching in an old kete, was that mad ngeru cat. Thomas.

She was heading for the shed up next to the road, where the river never reached. Tahuri wondered what Thomas would do to the chookies if he was locked in there with them too. Poor chookies.

Huh, she thought. Too much else to do. And bravely, she stepped out into the water and nearly lost her gumboots.

She could hear the other kids laughing and splashing and yelling, and she wondered whether to join them or stay and help Kui and just hang around home. Floods like this were such neat fun, at least for kids. But she hated the cleaning up afterwards, and going without a bath for weeks, and using the pakeha-style ones instead. Too small, those baths.

She splashed round the back to the chook house, but it was sad and wet and empty, the water boiling cold around the nests and clumps of sickly yellow straw and grey twigs snagged in the wire netting. The door hooked shut and she moved on, the chill sneaking through to her feet, gnawing at her toes.

Someone was yelling, over by the willow trees, that mass of knobby branches whipping across the water choked with floating rubbish. Terence was there in his tin boat left over from the summer, paddling up and down, proud of his corrugated rusty canoe made from the old toilet roof. He was yelling something about the pakeha's apple trees up the river – haw, haw, haw!

Tahuri hawed back, and went to find Kuikui.

She was there, on the other side of the house, planted firmly on the stump of an old sawn-down tree. Her face was lifted to the rain, drizzling faintly now, as it filled the brown furrows of her plump cheeks, and flubbed up her bifocals, which she wiped every now and then with a soft cotton cuff. Kui was wielding her garden rake, casting it out like a net, not letting it go, the pole handle confidently grasped. She was hooking in treasures – more than just the pakeha's sour green apples went bobbing by. Expertly, she snared and dragged in an almost new grey bucket, and again, a big red plastic clothes basket – very new, and she hadn't seen anything quite like that before. But mostly, Kui got sacks, and bits of fence, and branches full of unripe fruit, and bedraggled bits of clothing. One time, she had told Tahuri, she even got a ngeru; a wild little kitten, now Thomas the cat, safely locked up so he wouldn't float away again.

Kuikui loved it, out there, fishing for treasures in the rain. Hour after hour. For who knew what might come drifting by? And with even the smallest catch hauled in, a chuckle of pleasure blended with the rain. She also giggled at the ones that got away, though they were few.

Warm, back in the house, not caring about the flood any more because it stopped at the door step, Tahuri loved to watch her.

That's what it was like, the flood.

Uncle Ted In The Big Truck

Uncle Ted drives the Big Truck. Drives the Big Truck.
Uncle Ted in the Big Truck. By the Hospital Hill.
With the logs. Uncle Ted in the Big Truck.
Funny looking arm hangs out the window too.
Skinny on the end of a long tin stick. One on the
other side, poking from that window.
Turn left. Turn right. Goes the arm.
Uncle Ted in the Big Truck. Uncle Ted.
My Bedford. He says with a wide smile.
My Bedford. My Baby Girl.
With the logs on the Big Truck. Heavy. All piled
up. By the Hospital Hill.
 He leans out the window. Now. Big shoulder dark
like the logs. Long, too. Heavy.
Leans out and waves. From the Big Truck.
Not a high wave, or a sissy wave.
Not a wave like the Queen.
But a wave from the Big Truck. Like he's combing his
hair, but not quite. Just as far as his chin.
And he smiles, wide. While he leans out and waves.
At his niece on the side of the road.
Eyes popping out with pleasure.
Flapping her fingers madly at the Big Truck. There,
every working day.

Uncle Ted drives the Big Truck. Uncle Ted. In the
Big Truck. By the Hospital Hill. With the logs.

'Pity that one's not a boy,' he thinks.
And he leans out and waves.
From the Big Truck. By the Hospital Hill.

It Looks Pretty Dopey to Me

She didn't want to go home just yet. She didn't want to stay there either, because it was boring. But Cassina had made her go, like it was an excuse to go out, if she took her young cousin.

They were meant to be at the pictures, but had ended up with this Heke instead, in his father's car, and Tahuri was really pissed off. If she'd known that was Cassina's plan, she'd have said 'no dice'. But Cassina was a big girl and she wouldn't take much notice anyway, and just told her to come on stupid and shut up, and you tell Kuikui, and just see what you get, girl.

So she sat in the front seat of the '38 Chevvy while Cassina pashed up in the back with Heke, and made snuffling and snorting noises, and they both fogged up the windscreen like the mirror in the bathhouse. Fed up, Tahuri twiddled with the radio, her hero Elvis asked her if she was lonesome tonight. Yep. She was lonesome, and hoohaa, and bored.

Sometimes she'd have a sneaky jack, and Heke's half-bare bum would be stuck up in the air, and he'd be looking at her sideways, gulping with his mouth half open, and he'd gasp, 'Sina that fucken kid's watchin' us again. She's better off outside, eh?'

'Nah, Heke, come on hun. If we let her loose she'll run home and tell the old lady, you know . . .' That was for sure.

'Aw, c'mon Cassina. How can a man keep it up with that fucken kid watchin'?'

Cassina heaved herself up from underneath Heke's jacket, dense black curls frothing around her shoulders. Her bra was all screwed up, and a ripe plum nipple poked out, glistening. Heke sat up too, and pulled his shirt down over his front. Cassina leaned over, and fumbled around for her purse somewhere on the floor.

Tahuri wanted to giggle. She knew what was coming next.

'You go get us some smokes eh girl, and some lollies for you . . . And don't be too long, and make sure no one sees you 'cos we're meant to be at the pictures, eh . . .'

The brown ten shilling note crumpled in her hand. Tahuri slid out of the car and thankfully, silently, breathed in the freshness of the dark. Around her frost was falling, and sharp moonlight glittered through the trees. She went over to the swing and sat down, gazing out at Mokoia, bulky black upon the shimmering lake, and she thought about being in love. Behind her, the noises from the Chevvy were getting louder and louder, little high-pitched yelps, and deep gasping moans. All the windows were clouded up, heavy curtains. Tahuri set off for the corner shop.

They'd finished by the time she came back. Cassina was in the middle of the front seat again, next to Heke, whose arm was stretched across her shoulders. Hair clipped firmly back on her head, and red cardigan buttoned up neatly, she looked clean and prissy and nice, sitting there listening to the radio, hands folded around the taniko purse on her lap. Her knees sat primly together beneath the shaggy mohair skirt. Tahuri clambered in next to her, plonked the Craven As on the dashboard. She leaned her head against the sticky window.

Heke grinned a green toothy glow in the starter light. 'Better take you girls home, eh.'

The big Chevvy stopped at the top of the drive, rounded bumpers nuzzling gently into the thick, foggy steam. Tahuri swung the door open, heavy on the hinges. She leaped out, ran to the bathhouse. The slurping sounds of those two climbing into each other's mouths again competed with the sorrowful lyrics of 'Tell Laura I love her' turned up loud.

Kapai, the bath was in. And it was just right.

Checking that her towel was still on the rail, she quickly pulled off her clothes. Old black jersey basketball boots nylon socks blue jeans skivvie singlet underpants no bra yet thank god for that but something's on their way.

She slid gratefully into the soft waters.

'It's okay Hek, the old lady's asleep e! C'mon man – don't be a chicken!'

'You sure she's asleep now an' I'm no chicken either I jus' don' wan' us t'get caught, you know!'

'Okay then hurry up here and let me see the man you are. Neat one. Hey, you gotta match?'

Snappy match strike, and faint candle-light glimmered through the door. Tahuri was caught, she couldn't get out. She didn't want them to see her with nothing on. So she retreated into the farthest corner, safe in the darkness, wrapped in the steam. Her eyes bulging out of her head like a hapuka. She was going to see them doing it! Shit!

They looked as if they were glued together, as they lurched into the bathhouse, the wobbling candlestick dripping oily wax and long flame down the thick wool of Heke's jacket. Cassina was pulling at his clothes with her spare hand, the other bumping around looking for the ledge. She found it, plonked the candlestick down, and stuck herself back on to him again, dragging off his jacket and his shirt all in one smooth move. Her mohair skirt dropped to the floor too, revealing her small knees and rounded thighs rising up into the bare quivering brown cheeks of her bum. Expertly, she lifted her feet out of her louie heel, not moving an inch from where her front was squished tight up against his.

'Musta left her pants and stockings and stuff in the car,' flashed through Tahuri's mind, her eyes getting even bigger. 'And the bra, too.' Cardigan and blouse had joined the pile, and Cassina moaned, feeling Heke's spidery fingers move across her narrow shoulders, tussle the clips out of her hair, crawl slowly down her back to scoop each bum cheek like a fat watermelon, weighing, testing.

Their heads were hidden by the dark, but they looked as if they were eating each other's faces. And necks. And ears, too. Cassina worked at the belt while this was going on; she got the buttons undone, and with a lot of treading in one place, the jeans were down and trampled flat by two sets of feet.

Then one foot, small, high arched and dainty, flipped up into the air, and pushed its heel into Heke's waist. He moved her easily up against the wall, and started humping up and down really quickly, his body covering hers, so only his darkness shone dark brown, golden in the flickering candle-light. And they made a lot more noise, like in the car, only throatier and hoarser somehow.

Tahuri froze in the bath, clutched herself, still as a ponga tree. The shadows were large and black and crazy, their movement was going faster and faster, and Cassina's foot stayed where it was. This amazed Tahuri. Heke's bum was grinding away and his knees looked ready to buckle any minute. But his back was wide and proud and rippling, and Cassina's long slender hand stroked and explored. From the dark narrow crack at the bottom, to the huge bulk across the top; and down the roped and corded hardness of his flanks, the high ridged hollow of his spine. Slowly then quickly, slowly then quickly, her fingers danced. And Tahuri watched those fingers, fascinated.

Wow, she thought, pleased with herself. What a *neat* back. I'd love to have a back like that one day, and feel someone's fingertips playing with my muscles. That's what I want. Big muscles and a back like that and a girlfriend too. Just like that, that's what I want. To be like him. Yeah. To be like Heke.

She sighed, happy with her secret, and shut her eyes. She waited for them to finish. It was boring. They were going to do the same old stuff again.

A light went on outside. Suddenly, cutting through the steamy, frosty night. The back door creaked open.

'Tahuri! Are you out there? Where's that girl Cassina? Is she with Manu's boy?'

'Manu's boy' was Kuikui's name for Heke. Who pulled himself out in a huge hurry and planted his legs back into his pants.

'Shit, doll. I'd better shoot through!' Panic.

Cassina, in two swift, silent steps, was in the bath. Heke slid into the angle behind the door, dissolving into the darkness.

'E pai ana, Kuikui,' the older girl trilled. 'We're okay. Manu's boy's gone next door, and me 'n' Huri are in the bath now.' She paused, listening for a response. It came.

'Kapai, kare. I'll put the kettle on.'

The back door groaned shut.

'Hey Heke,' Cass whispered. 'See you tomorrow, eh?'

The young man, half dressed, carrying his boots and jacket, and hopping out to his car, didn't reply. Cassina wasn't worried by this, there was someone else on her mind.

'I wonder where that fucken kid is?' she said to herself.

'I'm here,' a small voice squeaked from the blackest, stillest corner of the bath.

Cassina rolled across the water, hurling a vast warm wave at Tahuri's face. She was sort of angry.

'You little shit!' she shrieked. 'You little creep! You watched us, didn't you! You watched us!' Then she laughed and laughed.

Tahuri lowered her chin down into the water. Her lips pursed, she blew little bubbly currents across the bath; they flittered around Cassina's bobbing heavy breasts.

'I always do,' she smirked. 'And it looks pretty dopey to me.'

Koura

Now was the part that Tahuri hated. But she had to do it, if she wanted to be with Kuikui tonight. She ran the long grass stem between her finger and thumb – it was still enough, and the end was sharp too, just right for the job. Clenching her jaw, and screwing up her nose, she pulled a wiggling dark red worm out of the tin. It danced and dangled, all sticky and wet and slimy. Promptly and without pity, Tahuri skewered it on the stalk, threading it all the way along. Then she picked up another, and another, until there was only a couple of inches of dry grass stem poking out at either end. So she started on the next one, and by the late afternoon, she had a slack, filthy heap of skewered worms for Kuikui to thread and knot carefully together, then tie on to the bamboo poles.

With her deft weaver's hands, Kuikui had the poles ready in no time, and they leaned up against the shed like floor mops outside the wharekai. But darker, and smellier, with their slender bamboo rods.

'Now we'll have some kai,' she smiled at her mokopuna, who was twitching with excitement. 'Haere mai, Huri. Come on.' Together, they went into her bach. And they waited for the moon.

She was rising high and silver above the willow trees as they walked down the river bank. Kuikui had the poles, and Tahuri clutched the big tin bucket in one hand, and a little raffia stool in the other. Both of them had rugs around their waists; winter was closing in; they were wearing big coats too, though the ngawha's bubbling warmth was only a few feet away. Kuikui propped the poles against the biggest willow tree and took the stool from Tahuri. Carefully, she positioned it on the very edge of the river bank. Gesturing to the child to spread her blanket next to the stool, she said not a word. Tahuri busily patted the blanket down and set the bucket between them. She knew that she wasn't going to sit on that rug though. Not likely! She'd be on her feet, and moving, if she had her way.

Kuikui settled on to her stool, arranging herself comfortably. She was so big and cushiony and warm, even on cool nights like this. Tahuri wanted to grab her and hug her, but they were too close to the water, and Tahuri didn't want them both to fall in. Especially Kuikui! Instead, she watched the old lady's face, and imagined the dappled moonshadows cast across her chin were like a moko, an old old pattern from another time; and she felt strange, with the willow leaves whispering and rustling around her head, and the sound of the river rippling by in long shining skeins of moonlight just below her feet. She saw Kuikui's lips were moving, and she stood very still, and then closed her eyes. It was a karakia – a prayer – it didn't take long. Then Kuikui murmured, in a low, meaningful voice, 'Homai tena, kare,' and Tahuri handed her the pole. All the worms were quite dead now, looped and coiled in crusty bundles.

Tahuri stayed very calm, and cautiously lowered her pole into the water, just a yard or so away from her grandmother's. Gently, she probed it against the bank, feeling the weedy willow rootlets growing in the mud. Like her kuia, she waited.

Something tugged at her pole. She wanted to screech with fright and joy. Quickly, she flicked the mucky pole end into the bucket – a stumpy shape like a chopped black finger squirmed in the tangle of worms; it fell with a clank to the bottom. Kuikui smiled at Tahuri; the young girl grinned back, and with her coat cuff covering her right hand, she picked it up and set it down in the grass. Swiftly, the thing scuttled sideways and with a plop! was back in the water again. Tahuri lowered her pole again, still looking at Kuikui. The old, sweet face creased quietly with pleasure.

'Ka pai, Tahuri,' her eyes said.

Over an hour passed. The bucket was almost full to the brim, clattering and clacking. They writhed and struggled to get out. Tahuri tried not to feel sorry for them – they were kai, after all.

No different from the wild pig her brothers brought home from the bush.

She walked over to the ngawha. A tukohu – cabbage tree kit – was hanging in its place from a knob in the apple tree, close to the steaming pool. She picked it up, twirled it in the air lazily, in huge arcs, like a big poi, moving easily beneath the moon. She reached her Kuikui and the bucket, and paused; the kuia nodded slightly. Tahuri stretched the mouth of the kete open as wide as she could, and rattled the bucket's contents into it. They clinked and glittered and fell, bundled up at the bottom of the bag, still thrashing, still resisting.

Taking no notice of them, Tahuri strode back to the ngawha. Dropped the tukohu in the boiling water, fastened its long plait to a stick hammered into the harder ground. Kuikui had said about five or ten minutes. She sat, inhaling the tasty, sweet-smelling steam, and watched a cloud slide over the moon. She waited. Fresh koura for supper when they got back to the whare. And for breakfast tomorrow. And maybe some to take to school for lunch. Saliva dripped around her teeth at the thought of them – soft luscious white flesh and those horrid little black snappy claws transformed into bright red delicacies so juicy to suck. Koura. What a treat.

But catching them was even better than eating them. Tahuri was convinced of that. Koura. And the full moon. And Kuikui. And the river. Koura.

Tahuri: the Runaway

'And I wonder where she will stay – ay
My little runaway . . .'

Tahuri clicked the radio off, watching the greyness of a bleak, bitter dawn slide through the curtain. She sighed, moved, sat up. She'd been lying on a raffia mat – her blanket had unwound, and her back ached where a work boot had squashed itself into her spine. She pulled it away, flung it out, then blinked around her. Wow! That's right! They'd done it – run away – they were free! Then she remembered the other things: the hazy struggles, her tearful, frightened shrieks – 'I'm only thirteen' – the spat retort like a glob of snot 'Little jailbait bitch, whatcha doin' here then, aye?' A blanket had been hurled against her, as she fell on to the floor. Where she stayed for what seemed hours, waiting, cowering, watching. Until the skinny, tattooed man had left, rattling off to work across the road like a lanky railway jigger, brumbling.

On the other bed, the full curves of her best mate Faye – soft pink flesh, a turned-up nose, thickly fanning eyelashes, plump lips whistling snores at the flyspeckled ceiling. Beside Faye, wedged against the wall, was another body, a dark curly head – one ear lobe daintily patterned with a five-pointed star, pierced through by a yellow ring. Shoulder pitted with pimples, right-hand fingers sprawling 'L–O–V–E' in a crooked line across it. Faye heaved, Tahuri immediately dropped back, then changed her mind, yawned, and dragged herself to the empty bed. She pulled off the reeking sheets and pillow case, rolled into the blanket, and shut her eyes. Another groan from the springs of the nearby bed. Tahuri thought, 'Oh no, not again.'

The young man scratched and grunted. Blankets, sheets, clothing mucked and muddled, Faye popped her large legs out,

Tahuri: the Runaway 35

freeing her friend nearby from his cramped position. Then she was on him. He squirmed, lurching, still half asleep. Straddled. The other girl gasped in her breath – tried not to giggle – Faye rocked to and fro enjoying herself hugely, grinding him down. He finally succumbed, gave a couple of half-hearted thrusts and scrawny groans. A muffled gurgle, more weakening grunts, then they were still. Quiet. Faye rolled off, beamed wickedly at the seemingly dozing Tahuri, then turned towards the wall. Her bed partner stood up, casually patted his prick with a grubby flap of sheet, then stretched into a stiff pair of jeans. With a quick glance at Faye's broad back, he approached the other bed. For a minute, he peered down at the frozen form, then wandered out.

'Hey, Faye!'
'What?'
'You 'wake? Has he gone now?'
'Yeah why? Didya see us?' (Giggle)
'Aw nah – not really. Hey whatsa time?'
'Bloody early. Go back to sleep.'
'But I'm hungry.'
'Then get an apple – outa the back pack over there. How are ya anyway?'
'I'm okay. Got a bit scared last night – I didn't like that Micky guy. He's horrible eh. I wouldn't let the creep near me. Lucky for him he didn't try too hard.'
'Yeah?' (Disbelief) 'God, Ta, you're such a kid. Hey! I think he's rather cute. You know, he's got a butterfly tattooed on his thing.'
'His *what*?'
'A butterfly! On his cock, you silly dumb bitch. Yeah! Neil was telling me – hard case eh! He says if he wants one, "How 'bout my butterfly go fly up your front passage?" Did he say that to you?'
'Ooh shit no! He believed me when I said I was thirteen – he left me alone then and laid off.'
'What! You stupid moll! Look, you're sixteen, I'm eighteen, see. Otherwise girl, we're in for it. Don't tell anyone your real

age 'cos they'll get the cops just like that and off we go. Don't you bloody dare try that again. Promise?'

'Yeah sorry Faye, I promise.'

'And don't forget, this was all your bloody mad idea, so let's make the most of it, okay?'

'Okay.'

She thought back – the hidings from her uncle, the bitchiness of her auntie. Always harping on about putting her in the Welfare. And that bloody awful top class full of stuck-up pakehas who laughed at her lunch, and talked about skiing all the time. How she swore she'd get away from it – escape, first to her big sister who lived in Auckland and could fix things up, then on home to her real mother, her real home. She knew her real mother was not very well, but Tahuri felt sure that it would be all right. Then something magic happened – she met Faye, who had the world – rich parents who adored her, two flash cars in the garage, a massive modern home with a swimming pool – and she'd done it, not just with boys, but with real men. One of her father's friends caught her alone in the shower, and they did it on the bathroom floor, and then on her parents' bed too! Faye was special. She had really been around, she was one hell of a mate, and Tahuri was rapt. Just wild about her. She had guts, and good looks, and all she had to do now was run away from home. And that would be it – she'd done everything. And on to a new life – free!

They had arranged to meet at the main intersection on the Friday night. Tahuri was there, midnight on the dot. Waited for an hour. Knew that Faye wasn't going to turn up. Decided, right, I'll go and get the scrubber. Jogged down to her friend's house, then with a quick pocket-knife in the lock, was creeping along the Bartletts' wall-to-wall carpet. Within minutes, she was by her friend's bed. Poor Faye nearly shit her sheets. But she didn't chicken out. And so they were off. That was when the rain started. Buckets of it. They were no sooner on the road, than the clouds emptied over their bare heads. Neither had thought about rain. Drenched and miserable, stubbornly not talking, they trudged on. A big white Holden pulled up. 'Hop in girls!' And they were on the way to Hamilton. The driver dropped them at a place Faye had been raving about for weeks. The Hotel Edinburgh, the railway workers' hostel.

Faye was snoozing now. Tahuri got up slowly, munching the apple. What a bloody dirty hole of a place! She hadn't noticed the smell, but now it was bad. Dragging on another jersey, she crept through the door, and shut it quietly. It was about seven thirty – still too early for a Saturday – what was she going to do? Oh hell. Faye had giggled something about 'cracking it for some cash'. Oh well, Faye could do what she liked. Although that sounded a bit off to Tahuri. Anyway . . .

The corridor was long and bare, and damply brown. A door opened. Standing there was a youngish man, wearing a white towel, clean jeans and a snowy singlet. He smiled, they started talking, he asked her into his room . . . well, they could be cousins, she considered. His name was Thomas, and he came from a 'real hick place, way up the river'.

They laughed together, worked out that they did have relations in common – he said he was twenty-six, engaged and a working man. Then he warned her not to leave his room until he came back from the job because the hostel was no place for a young girl. He promised to look after her, but she had to stay put in his room. He took a stack of comics and magazines from under the bed, and put them on the bed. Then 'See you at four, Huri –' and leaving more orders to be careful, he shut the door and was gone.

His place was nice to sit in – photos of sturdy football teams and calendars on the wall, a navy blue and white pennant pointing 'Auckland' at the lino-covered floor. A taniko belt hung by its buckle from a nail, which tacked a floral curtain across a corner to make a wardrobe. A little table with a radio and flowers had trays on it – more photos, this time of relations and a wedding, with Thomas the best man. A stubby chest of drawers was at the bottom of the bed. She noticed his room didn't seem to stink like the other one.

Tahuri read some comics, soon got bored with Spiderman,

and fiddled with the radio. She thought about Faye. What if she really was cracking it? Whatever that meant.

She had to find out. She rushed out the door, thumped down the hall to the rat hole. No Faye. Only a big blond guy rifling through their bags.

'Hey!' she growled. 'Who are you? Those are my gears!'

He snorted back, 'Wow, but I like this transistor. Yours, is it?'

'No, it's my mate Faye's.'

'Oh well – what's it worth if I say it's mine now?' He edged over to her, kicking the door closed. She stepped back. He chuckled, cradling the machine. 'Well, Spear-thrower?'

Tahuri sniffled – 'Oh, have the bloody thing, I don't care!' then squeezed through the door. The voice behind her laughed. 'Spear-thrower,' it echoed.

As Tahuri paused to catch her breath, she heard the familiar sighs and snorts of Faye, getting into it again. Confused, wanting Faye, needing a cuddle, she walked back to Thomas's.

'And what the hell are you doin' here, blackbitch?'

A voice coarse as railway grit croaked down at her. Tahuri blanked out for a moment, gaping.

'I'm just looking for my cousin Thomas Whitireia – he lives here, eh?' She did her best to look like an innocent teenager, and not a mad runaway.

'Yeah, but he's away till four. Y'can wait in the dining-room for 'm. One o' my girls in there. Mind you, I don't like your kind of women around here, it's not good. Relations or not. Well, Tom might be in for lunch –' She waddled off.

Tahuri was dazed. The woman was pumpkin squat, a smeared grey apron roped across a patchy tartan skirt, her legs bloating painfully into purple scuff slippers. Massive arms, a red wrinkled neck, tiered beneath a florid face. Pulpy yellow curlers squirmed about her grey skull like stuffed rubber maggots. A flaring scar slashed across her cheek, under her right ear, and her left profile showed decades of gouges and weathering, powder-flaked and patterned with finely broken blood vessels. She looked over her shoulder, grimaced, and was gone.

The girl turned into the kitchen. More smells. Dishes – stinking, unwashed heaps covered the stove and table. The floor was strewn with vegetable peelings, dirt, dog-chewed bones. On the coal range, two large pots farted forth, and the flaking enamel fridge held its door shut with a rubber band.

Below the fridge, a pile of rubbish swarmed greedily with blowflies – bottles, ashes, egg cartons, cans, food scraps, butts, and more curling vegetable skins – Tahuri was glad she had shoes on, and headed for the dining-room.

It was quite ordinary, just as gloomy as the rest of the Edinburgh. A huge self-set table, scattered with bits of leftover breakfast, and very heavy old furniture. On one armchair sat a young man, earnestly reading the paper. Opposite him, a very pregnant girl, tired and sallow, was knitting something fluffy. She did not look up at all. Tahuri twitched, noticed the youth. 'Hello,' she stuttered. 'That landlady told me to come in here ... ummm ... I ... umm ...'

'Hi,' a flash of green eyes from the yellow armchair. The pregnant knitter said nothing. Tahuri felt shy, retraced her way out. The young man grinned. 'See you later!' he called.

Feeling rather stupid – and wondering if the boy had anything to do with that girl in there – she sneaked back to Thomas's. Bad luck – the door had slammed shut, locking the key in and Tahuri out. And he wasn't coming back for lunch. So she had time on her hands. For what? She checked her pockets, pleased to feel some cash, and feeling again that sweet smell of freedom, she strolled across the street.

Across the way, the railway junction, burgundy burnt and black and porous stones, ruddy, heat-blasted carriages, grimy ribbed containers, interlocked and lacing steel. And everywhere, the sense, the excitement of people, of things, going places far away. Going somewhere else. Tahuri thrilled at this, pushed her hands deeper into her pockets, smiled at the ugliness of the junction town that widened around her as she climbed the overbridge. She felt good. She looked over the neat red roofs of railway houses, row upon row; she took in the green, spreading flourish of the town along the riverbank. And just across from the bridge, she studied the bleak pink doss-house – the Hotel Edinburgh.

Suddenly she spotted a figure on the verandah, playing a big guitar. Making out she didn't care anyway, she shambled aimlessly back to the hostel . . . She was right, it was that guy in the dining-room. Her heart thumped, but it didn't matter. After all, she was free!

'Hi there. Whose your name?' Long fingers snaked across the glossy Astoria.

'Tahuri. I'm looking for my cousin Thomas Whitireia. You know him?'

'Shit yeah. He never said anything about you. Sneaky, all right. Anyway, I'm Jackie. Jackie Farnham. Like to come in my room for a while?'

Those green eyes flashed again, and Tahuri felt funny.

He sprang quickly off the verandah ledge and pushed the guitar into her arms. Then he was over the windowsill and inside.

'This is where I live,' he smiled, charming. 'Come in, listen to the radio eh?'

Tahuri peered in. 'Aw, no,' she giggled. 'Better not, eh.'

'Why not?' He seemed put out. 'Nothing's gonna happen to you. Hey, aren't you one of the chicks who came in last night?'

She blushed at this – he knew about her, maybe he'd been asking around, finding out who she was.

'No, Jackie. I'm okay out here, really –'

'Oh shit,' he snarled. 'C'mon babe, come in – don't lead a man on, eh.'

'Look, Jackie, I –'

'D'you want me to come out and get you then! Cos I'm fucken goin' to, you cheeky cunt!'

He was through the window. She was in his arms, kicking and squawking. What the hell was going on? Somehow he managed to get both their bodies back into the room, then he tossed her on the bed, slammed the window down, bolted it. Tahuri gazed up at him, gulping. He was very methodical. He drew the tatty black holland blinds, checked the window catches, motioned her to a chair. She obeyed. He then moved the wardrobe against the door, and the bed against the window. Then running his lean hands over his chest, flexing his well-muscled arms, he just peered at Tahuri. He seemed very tall, very massive; his body glinted light copper, and excitement pulsed visibly against the fly on his jeans. He moved. Scooping the girl up, he stretched her on the bed, roughly handling her body which seemed frozen stiff and struck dumb by all his attention. He unzipped his pants, loosened hers, pulled at them, groping at the patch between her legs. At this, she reeled way, gasping, 'No, no, Jackie – don't. Please stop, I'm only thirteen, I've never done this, no, no, please stop . . .' He was deaf, his hands and heavy body working at her madly. She began to struggle – he now realized that she was jailbait for sure, and belted her head, tore into her rocking body with a swelling urge. Tahuri bucked and howled – her terror increased at the sound on the door – a hefty hammering – 'Hey Jackoboy save some for us eh, haw haw haw –' She screamed, wildly biting at him; he furiously slammed himself somewhere against her hip bone. She thrashed and shrieked, he growled, kept hitting her head, as she clawed at his ears and neck and hair. Pushing down, thrusting hard. With a gasp, he jerked fiercely, quickly, sighed, then fell back, pushing her on to the floor. Globs of white goo oozed down her thighs, messed thickly in her bruised, sticky hairs . . .

'Here she is, boys – take her, she's a fucken tiger!'

Next thing, thrown across the corridor into a larger, open, well-lit room – four beds, four crawling, mauling, clumsy apes all ripping at her clothes – Tahuri fought and fought – she went down, a face lunged near hers. There was a cross tattooed above the right eyebrow. Through dry tears, she noticed an alarm clock on the bedside table. She forced an arm free – one youth held her arms, the others were at her legs, tugging at her jeans, making it easier for the straining face above her. She clenched her teeth, her free arm grabbed the clock, swung, brought it down on the face, on the tattooed cross –

A yowl – four shocked youths – enough time to wriggle up and out towards the window.

'I'm bleeding! My eye! My eye's bleeding! The fucken bitch – I'm bleeding, I'm bleeding –'

The window was open. Not caring what was on the other side, Tahuri hurled herself out and ran. She didn't look back for at least four blocks. Then falling into a spongy green hedge, soft in an empty street, she cried.

What the hell was she going to do now? Her clothes were stained, torn and splattered – her shirt hung in bits, the front ripped across and the waist of her jeans was jagged from the zip almost to her knee. She needed some clothes. Suddenly she had the answer. Clotheslines! That's what she had to do. She followed the hedge, stealthily scouting for the right back yard. There it was – an old house, a well-stocked line, no dogs, no fences. Jeans, shirts, jerseys flapped lazily in the cool wind. Watching the house, she dashed silently out, grabbed the stuff gleefully, and then lay flat down under the springy arms of the hedge. No underpants; too bad. On her back, she swiftly squirmed into her newly acquired gear. And then she stood up, feeling much better. But a bit cold, and very sore. Rolling her own clothes up into a ragged bundle, Tahuri headed back to Frankton, as if nothing had happened.

Avoiding the hostel, she noticed the time on the railway clock – 3.45, almost time for Thomas to finish work. He'd be really wild if he knew. What was there to do? Think about it. She went into a small dairy jammed between a draper's and a furniture shop. The shop assistant, very prim and proper, gave her a funny look. Tahuri hoped she hadn't pinched the old bag's clothes, then thought it hardly likely. Leaning against the window, and watching the pub across the road, she sipped her Coke, ignoring all the passersby who seemed to gawk at her. It was then she noticed herself – her hands and arms, bloodstains and caked scratches, fingernails cracked and torn. And her head, dully throbbing, was sore in the places where their blows had cut through, matted hair tangled in sticky knots. She realized her body was clammy with sweat, blood, and sperm; she tried not to feel sick, stood up straight, and cool, and ready, and confident.

A pair of middle-aged men in overalls lurched out of the pub, clutching their take-home flagons. Then through the door, and down the steps, tumbled a couple, the woman wobbling and noisy, falling on the man who jerked leerily up the path – it was Faye! And that horrible Micky. Tahuri was on them.

'Faye! I've been lookin' for you all bloody day!'

'Oooh haha my little mate . . . where've you been, sweetness? C'mon dearie we're goin' back to the Ed, eh Mick sweetheart?' The man scowled, said nothing, stayed sullen. Faye gaped.

'Oooh – you been in the wars dearie? Y'got blood all over you . . .'

'Oh god Faye, fuck it –'

'Yes please . . . Had any yet?' The bleary mascara clotted eyes lit up.

'Nah, nah, nothing.' Sniff. Smile. 'Hey, I'll come back with you, eh.'

Thomas was on the verandah, arms tensely folded, eyes glowering. Tahuri felt confused – he crossed over to her, put his arm around her shoulder, took her bundle of clothes. She began to sob. Deep and long and racking. The other two looked on, blinking and drunk, they hobbled off down the hallway.

Back in his room, Thomas fed Tahuri handkerchiefs and hot flannels, and tried to comfort her. Apparently the boys were sorry – they were just being mad, crazy, weren't really going to hurt her, he went on.

At this, Tahuri snapped back between snivels, 'Bullshit! Fucken bullshit, Thomas! They knew all along, they meant to do me over, the bastards! And that Farnham creep really tried! Oh –' But Thomas kept on, trying to comfort her, while quietly insisting that the boys wouldn't treat a Maori girl, one of their own, like that. They just wouldn't. But he didn't say a word about Farnham, and he didn't mention how he had told Tahuri to be careful, and stay in his room.

The door rattled with impatient knocking. Tahuri jumped.

'It's Mick,' muttered Thomas, opening the door a little. 'Yeah?'

'Gotta get this bloody kid outa here. And that mad nympho Faye. The place is bloody red hot –'

'But we can't leave now, it's still daytime –'

'Yeah, I know. Wait until it's dark, then shoot through, okay? You take her, and I'll take the other one.'

'Onslow Street?'

'Yeah – Norma's place. It's cool around there. Then we'll work out what's next.' The door shut, Mick was gone. Thomas turned, faced Tahuri.

'Well, little sister, it looks like you'll be back on the road. But you just make sure you get to your sister's place all safe and sound, okay? No more trouble on the way.'

After the day's happenings, Tahuri was quick to agree. But what about Faye?

Thomas grinned, slow and sly. 'That girl will manage wherever there are men around, Tahuri.' He looked at his watch. 'You hungry?'

'Yeah – well, no, I mean –'

'Don't worry, I never eat anything that comes from that repo in the kitchen either. I'll get one of the boys to get some kai from up the road –' He slipped out the door.

Tahuri heard guitar picking, faintly, down the hall. Then it stopped. The door was ajar. She swallowed, felt the bruises flaring on her thighs. Bastard. Crept over to the door, pushed it firmly –

'Hey, Ta, it's all right girl, it's only me, Thomas –' She relaxed, curled back against the wall, cushioned by a pillow.

'We're having smoked fish and oysters and chips and kukus – Arapeta's going to get it, just to prove how sorry he is.'

'Arapeta?'

'The one you gave that beaut black eye. You cut his eyebrow clean in half, you could've blinded the poor bugger you know. If you swung that thing any harder –' There was pride in his voice, he was pleased. For the first time in ages, she felt good.

'Good job,' she snorted, satisfied. 'I wish I had –'
But Thomas was busy, clearing away the small chest at the foot of his bed, spreading out great sheets of the *Times*, balancing a half-empty bottle of scarlet tomato sauce on a picture of prize-winning pigs at the A & P show. The table ready, he produced some glasses from his bottom drawer, wiped them gleaming with a tea towel from the same place. For him, the subject of what had happened that afternoon was best left alone. Forgotten – or put away somewhere. You never fixed anything up by talking about it. Not stuff like that.

Footsteps, a delicious chippy takeaway smell, meant food was on the way. Thomas went to the door. Words were exchanged. The parcel passed hands; the youth outside walked back to his own room. Thomas shut the door with his elbow, piled the steaming package on the rugged tablecloth. They ate, talked, until both noticed at the same time how dark it was outside. Time to move. Thomas found her gear. They bundled up the greasy newspapers, drained their glasses, and once again were back in the hall where they had met that same morning, years of hours ago. With no one around, they were on their way.

River fog and rain thickened the air; the night was crawling with damp and cold. To Tahuri, it seemed that they walked, and walked, and bloody walked. Side-roads, alleys, railway tracks, schools, back yards, even a rugby grandstand. Then they came to a busy main road.

'And here we are,' grunted Thomas, breath gulping in steamdrifts.

Just another ordinary-looking little house across the road. Drab, old, grey, behind a ragged fence. Hedge on one side, stubbly drive on the other, with a ramshackle garage fringed with frostbitten hydrangeas.

They went around the back, walked into a large dining-room. A kerosene space heater gave off an evil-smelling warmth; bottles, cans, glasses, ashtrays, cards and assorted rubbish scattered across the table. Plates of half-eaten food were pushed into a corner, a grimy nest in a pile of pie and chip packets, and a stealthy fox terrier-cross lurked and licked its way around the floor. Faye and Mick were fumbling around half-dressed on a bulbous armchair.

'Hiya kid,'.Faye chortled. 'Whosya friend?' She rose clumsily, plopped back with a hairy hand planted on her waist. Tahuri was struck dumb – couldn't think of what to say. Out of the blue, Thomas asked, 'Mick, which room, brother?'

'The one on the right.'

Tahuri froze up. Oh no. Not again. Thomas gently pressed her hand.

'It's okay, Tahuri.' He made soft reassuring noises. 'I won't do anything –' Dimly, Tahuri recalled Jackie murmuring those same words, just as gently. She pulled back, looked wildly around her. Thomas tightened his grip on her arm, fixed her against the wall.

'Tahuri,' he sounded angry. 'I'm not going to try anything, I'll be out there with the others, you'll be okay. You've gotta get some sleep, now try. I'll come in later, and see if you're okay. You'll be all right here, girl. Now settle down.' A brotherly kiss on the forehead, and he was gone.

Tahuri drowsed for what seemed hours. Suddenly, the door lurched open, and Thomas staggered in, a girl tittering behind him. He shook Tahuri awake. 'Hey Bubs.' He was breathing whisky and beer. 'Yah gotta go into the other room with Carol. You'll be okay, just go in, she's all by herself. Norma's back, so me 'n hers having her room, eh doll –' he drooled to the tall girl who yelped skittishly as his hand slid under her sweater. Tahuri got up, saying nothing. Scowling at Thomas, who tottered uneasily beside the bed, she pushed her way out of the room and plonked down to the next one.

The naked light bulb exposed a large, untidy space – a sofa, three shabby armchairs, a dark coffin wardrobe and matching dresser, and against the wall nearest the door, a set of bunks. Tahuri also noticed a bed – big double mattress on a legless spring base – in the middle of the room, covering much of the stained and patchy carpet. She didn't like the look of the bed, and seeing the upper bunk was occupied by a small shape, she made for the lower one. After she'd remade it, she wandered over to the light switch by the door. A husky voice followed her.

'Hi, you must be Tahuri. Heard about you from that mad bag Faye. I'm Carol.' Tahuri returned the other girl's curious look. She had sat up, to lounge bare-shouldered across the top of the bunk. Her face was young, traces of make-up smudged around her eyes, and all the colour had been licked off her lips, leaving a subtle outline. This Carol was really interesting. Tahuri smiled back, pleased to make a new friend.

'Yeah, that's right. D'you want the light out?'

'Okay. But keep the small one on, over there by the wardrobe.'

Carol watched the younger girl with half-closed eyes. Tahuri returned to the bunk, considering whether to leave on her jeans or take them off. At that moment, Carol leaned over the bunk, her breasts falling creamy and full before Tahuri's amazed eyes. Her face was upside-down and laughing, and her hair, spilling everywhere, was brown and silky. She smirked.

'Well, dummie? You gotta come up here, didn't you know? Ian sleeps on the bottom bunk, and Mick and Faye will be on the big one later. Ha. So come on up.' She retreated, thin legs extended over the edge.

'And you can take off those damn jeans.' Her voice was commanding.

Tahuri climbed the ladder on to the top bed. Carol's body snaked beneath the sheets. She was smiling. Not knowing what to do, the younger one hesitated, curled at the other end. Somehow she felt threatened. But not in a horrible way. Oh, no. Not like that.

Carol lay stiff and tense, then leaped up, giggling. Tahuri jumped, her head slamming clunk against the ceiling. Shit. This was too much.

'C'mon, hon,' Carol purred across at her. 'I don't bite. Promise. It's more comfortable down here by me. The bunk's damn well narrow enough without you playing silly buggers over where you're gonna sleep.' She blinked at Tahuri in the dimpled light, the sheet dropped to reveal her well-made breasts and tight belly. She flopped back on the pillows and stretched out a pale arm.

The dark girl fought back her feelings. This was weird, she felt really randy, sort of excited, like something great was going to happen. All tight down there. Almost sore. Hoping for some reason that Carol was naked only from the waist up, she slid her legs under the sheet, and plunked her head on the pillow. Then it hit her – bare, smooth legs – no pyjamas.

Tahuri couldn't help but admire Carol's shape, especially where her hip rose up from her waist in a long graceful line under the sheet. And her back was so smooth . . . She lay staring at the quietly breathing Carol, started to feel the cold of her loose-fitting cotton shirt. She began to shiver, then abruptly rolled over and bunched up, clamping the pinkly filtered lamplight from her eyes.

Carol stirred behind her, a hand crept daintily over her waist, drew her into a close embrace. Warmth. She fitted perfectly, moved sneakily, quietly, so that hardened nipples pecked into her flesh. She felt another hand part the hair of her neck, and fluffy, light kisses on her skin. Tahuri stiffened – the fingers at her waist tightened, locked across her midriff. Trembling, she clutched them in her fist. The kisses stopped. Carol whispered urgently, furtively.

'Tahuri, darl, relax. Don't worry, it's only me, I won't do anything, honest – I mean, I don't wanna upset you, hon, it's just that I thought, well, you know –'

Tahuri turned over, loosening Carol's hand. She was completely mixed up. It was crazy. Fantastic. Yet she felt like she'd never felt before, ever. Aroused, randy, free, and relaxed about it. Roughly, she forced her arms around Carol's slim body, then pressed herself purposefully against her, coiling her legs around the other's, pushing her against the wall. The rest just happened. She felt slow and at ease, sure and gentle, flowing ... eventually, she fell into a dense and dreamless sleep, sharing the warmth and comfort of Carol's body.

Carol had gone when Tahuri woke up. It was early morning – she remembered the night before, and felt strange. But really good about it. She wondered where everyone had gone – the other beds had obviously been used; bedclothes tossed and tousled all over the room. Stiff and very sore from the previous day, she dragged herself down, pulled on her clothes, then went out into the kitchen. There, looking quite apart from it all, was the same pregnant girl, still knitting.

'Outside,' she snarled a brief answer to Tahuri's unspoken question.

Tahuri walked out into the yard. Thomas's voice barked at her – 'Watch out, Ta! Come over here!' She hurried over to him, then saw why he had shouted.

Micky was in the middle of the scrubby back yard, balancing an axe. The tip of the handle was poised delicately between his palms, swinging rhythmically, gathering momentum. At exactly the right moment, he released it, tossing it high into the air, where it reeled two, three, four times, then thunked down blade first into the ground. It was a craftier, more dangerous form of knife throwing.

Thomas had his turn, skilfully spinning it higher and further. Carol and Norma both clapped, twittering congratulations. Faye, not the centre of attention, frowned beneath her hangover. She nodded at Tahuri, who grinned shyly at Carol. Beautiful Carol, who looked different, almost colourless, in the daylight.

'Gidday, darl,' she half sighed. 'Let's go have some coffee, eh. You coming in, Faylay?' She signalled to Mick, who checked the axe's swing. Together the four females went into the house.

Thomas followed them in, announcing that he was off to get them tickets to Auckland. Faye grunted, her eyes bloodshot, peering angrily from puffy sockets. Tahuri wondered why the pupils were so wide, so wild. Hoped Faye wasn't sick; hoped

even more that she could catch some time with Carol, and get to
know her better. Maybe she was feeling ashamed – or maybe
she was playing it cool.
 Norma jangled the coffee cups, and Faye dozed conveniently,
her head lolling on her arms, bent on the table top. The knitter
was nowhere to be seen. Carol moved closer to Tahuri, bent
down as if to pick something up from the floor near the feet.
Playfully, slowly, ran her fingertips over the bare brown toes,
caressing each nail, teasing the skin, one by one . . .
 Tahuri felt that weird tingling, grabbed Carol by the neck,
pulled her down, gasping.
 'Fuckit Carol, Norma's just out there, and Faye's not asleep –'
 'Aw, c'mon darl, you'll be gone soon –'
 'Dammit! Shit! What'll we do –'
 Suddenly the front door began to rattle with heavy-handed
knocking.
 Faye was instantly awake and alert, making her way to the
back of the house. Cursing, Carol peered cautiously through a
side window. The knocking kept on.
 'Shit oh dear,' she glanced at Tahuri. 'Fucken cops. You'd
better go out the back now, hon, quick! Faye knows where,
hurry up!'
 Tahuri whipped through the kitchen and bowled into Faye
who yanked her into a built-on shed. It was a huge cupboard full
of empty coal sacks. Mick prodded Faye in, then bolted it shut.
And very casually, like a man with all the time in the world, he
strolled down to the front door. After a brief talk, his callers
left, unconvinced and frustrated.

The hiding place was stuffy. Tahuri fought down her sneezes
but couldn't complain about the coal dust. She resented the
thick press of Faye's body, with Micky's smells, wrapping itself
around her. Just in time, the bolt slid out, the two scrambled on
to the floor.
 Back in the kitchen, Micky leaned on the rear legs of his
chair, glaring at Faye as they came in.
 'When Tom comes back, you two are off, okay?'

'Okay,' she half simpered, trying to be tough. He got up, grabbed her, and they were down the hall again, and into Norma's bedroom.

Tahuri stretched out against the wall, looked longingly at Carol.

Minutes passed. Carol said something about the coffee they hadn't been able to finish. Tahuri agreed. Norma announced she was going for a walk. They were both staring rather awkwardly into their coffee mugs when Thomas marched in, looking very business-like and pleased with himself. He presented the railcar tickets to Tahuri.

'You'll be okay, Bubs,' he sounded encouraging. 'I'm sorry about last night. That's why you have to get out of here, and the sooner the better. Try and see your sister as soon as you get there.' He then handed her a wad of carefully folded notes. 'Sorry it's not more . . .'

The goodbyes were short and silent. They decided to walk to the station. Thomas took them half-way, then planted a quick kiss on Tahuri's cheek, and was gone into the night. Faye, freshly spruced up and ready for another night of action, was anxious, excited, turned on by the thought of a bigger city, brighter lights. She didn't feel pushed out, oh no, she felt pushed forward, moving on to something better, something more than Rotorua or Hamilton could ever be. With a mission, she walked on, hips swinging, breath steaming, eyes flashing at the shadows.

Tahuri silently trailed her, her head full of Auckland and Carol and Jackie Farnham, his hard viciousness and cruelty, his hate; of Carol's yielding softness and warmth, her pleasure. It was all quite mad, she was beginning to think. Mad, whichever way you looked at it. And as for those other dogs, shit . . .

A light green late model Ford pulled over to the curb. The door swung open, a smooth, oily voice crooned at Faye,

'Hi there, lovely. How's business?'

Tahuri held back – something was not quite right here. But Faye softly purred her response,

'Super, sweet.' She leaped into the car, then grimaced. 'One little problem – what about *her*? She's sort of my sister –'

The man looked thoroughly evil. 'Oh, bring her along too. She can watch!' He motioned to Tahuri, who crammed herself next to Faye. Who snapped at her, 'It's okay. The train goes in an hour, dummie,' as she started to work on the man's fawn polyester thigh.

Tahuri watched the trees slide by, gross, intriguing shapes in the fog. She broke the silence.

'Where are we going?'

'Don't worry sweetheart, you'll see.'

More corners, long, wide streets, the rise and fall of the road, and the rain-slicked dazzle of oncoming cars. All of a sudden they stopped.

They were outside a gaunt, grey stone building, very badly lit. A blue-lettered sign glowed glumly above the door.

'Well, Misses Bartlett and Amokura.' The man smiled for the first time since he had picked them up. Beaming, he slid out of the car, and gestured at the weeping concrete steps. 'Will you come this way, please?'

Paretipua

Came out of the whare. Stood on the step, big and strong. Paretipua. Hair wrapped in a towel. From the bath, from the steam. Hair wrapped in a towel, dark dark blood dark red towel. Wrapped up. On top of her head. Paretipua. Came out of the whare.
Shoulders bare, and wide, and brown, deep colour, glossy. Deep colour too on her cheeks, on her face, on her chin.
Bright eyes flashing and sweet kind smile. Sweet kind smile and white white teeth. And fingernails, too.
Sweet kind smile, bright eyes flashing. Paretipua. Came out of the whare. Hair wrapped in a towel. Shoulders bare.

Across the Ruapeka, dawn glittering feebly through the steam.
Slowly, the sun rose; shadows crept like blots upon the water; tree branches twisted, and the raupo stretched and rustled, wiry thin.
The woman paused at the doorway, welcoming the morning, herself stately as the sun. She balanced the heavy towel on her head, looked around, noticed her small niece, the quiet, queer one, setting the breakfast pots down near the ngawha. She smiled. At the little girl. At the promising, preening sun. She smiled.

Paretipua. Shoulders bare and wide and brown, deep colour, glossy. Lifted her arms up. High, elbows high. Bent her head over. Head with hair wrapped in a towel. Dark dark blood dark red. Bent her head over, arms up. And fingernails, too. Paretipua.
Towel undone. Hair spilled out, black, black. Falling, falling. Falling down, falling. From shoulders bare and wide and

brown. Black hair, black. Long. Thick. Long. Waves of black.
Long hair, dyed muka ropes, dried by the sun.

Black, black. Waves of black. Falling, falling. Paretipua.

She flexed her shoulders, turned her neck, swung around, and
the heaviness of her hair spilled almost to the step. The weight
of it. Yet she could never cut it, not freely, this gift she wore like
the finest cloak; it meant too much, for too many people. So
instead, she enjoyed it. The wonder, the blackness, the weight.
And the beauty. Steadying her feet, bending forward slightly,
knees spread, hand clasping thighs, she tossed it to the sunlight,
to the morning; a cloak, a fishing net, a cloud of lustrous black.

Waves of black. The wonder. Sparkling and shimmering,
black, black, caught in the sunlight, water stars, shimmering
and sparkling.

Water stars, made by the hair, caught in the sunlight, black,
black.

Falling, falling. Sparkling and shimmering, water stars,
water stars. Black, black. And water stars.

From the sunlight. From the morning.

From the shoulders bare and wide and brown. From the
waves of black, black. The wonder. From the morning.

From her. Came out of the whare. From Paretipua.

Old Man Tuna

She pulled the laces tight on her shoes, eyes scanning the riverbank. Vague shapes in the steam. Her brothers were still there – not quite waiting for her, but still there. That was the main thing. Although she wanted to, she didn't yelp with delight. She had promised to shut up and be quiet, so that she didn't scare away the fish. The fish, the fish. Much more important than her, a mere girl, who was just a nuisance anyway. Though she could have her uses. Maybe.

They were still ahead, but she could see them; large, dark shapes gliding through the shadows. Big guys. Milton was nineteen, and had a motorbike and a pakeha girlfriend. He told spooky kehua stories that made your skin tingle and go all stiff like a dead chicken's, while his eyes got bigger and bigger and glowed like headlights. Scary and horrible. But Milton was fun too; he always brought home Cadbury Roses chocolates for his sister and Bailey's Irish Cream for the old lady, who loved him. She hadn't met the girlfriend yet; plenty of time for that, he reckoned. His brother, Tuku, wasn't so sure. He was always thinking – never said much, read his books and looked out of the window most of the time. No motorbike for him; he had his sights set on a Citroen. Style. That was his secret, as he moved through the rustling bushes in his uncle's old swandri and grandfather's frayed-out cords. Style, that's Tuku, graceful as a preening cat. Clutched in his left hand, the cold smoothness of an AFFCO meat hook. His eel gaff.

The moon was on her back, and pale light dripped feebly down between the weeping willow branches. They stopped. They were there – at the place; barely ten minutes walk from home. Too close, thought Whero.

'Here's fine.' Milton lifted his rod and flexed it lovingly. 'Got that big one last night, just about this spot. Let's try her out again, e bro?'

The younger brother nodded. Both men stretched, and shrugged, then set to fixing their gear.

Whero watched, squatting in a pool of darkness, her elbows wrapped around her knees. So much for her big outing with the boys. It was boring; even the place was wrong; if she climbed up a nearby tree, she could see the lights at home; if she really stretched her neck she could see right into the sitting-room, past the lace curtains. And there would be Kuia, happily watching TV, blue haze flickering across her gentle face. Whero had hoped they'd walk for miles, all the way to the mouth of the river. What a bummer.

She stood up. Whispered. 'Hey, Milt, can I go for a walk?'

Whirr, whirr, whirr went the reel. Whirr, zipzipzip. 'Okay. Not too far.'

'I won't. I'll just go down a little bit. Not far.'

'When I whistle, you come back, girl.' Zipzip, whirr.

'Yeah, I will.' She glanced at Tuku, who was crouching like a river stone, absolutely still. Gaff at his side. String line between finger and thumb of right hand. He was at it again. Thinking.

She felt marvellous – free! Out in the night air! She danced quietly along the track, breathing in the darkness and faint moon-gleam, running her fingertips through a wall of flax. Paused as the track opened on to a scrubby bank. Dense grass fringed and dripped into the river; the water looked dark, a solid oily mass of black, punctured with melting globs of light. Out of the water, a raupo clump tufted shivering; some spines drooped sadly, streaming in a greasy line around an ancient log, which formed a ragged, festering bulk to the shore. Threatening, choked in a slime of thick weed.

Whero stopped. She knew this place – how different it looked at night! Worse even than in the daytime. Spooky. The water, so still. Where the old man tuna lived, they said. Somewhere in that weed. In the willow stump. Or underneath the log. A Big One.

'Yuk,' she thought. Strained her ears. Whirr, whirr.

Everything was normal, okay. If he whistled, she'd hear. If she shrieked, he'd hear. Both of them would. And her own favourite place, where she liked to be and doze and think, was close by, just a little bit further along. Where the water trickled again.

Behind her, in the dark weeds, something moved. Broke the water, like a boneless ebony arm. It rose smoothly, gleaming, from the ooze. Then fell into it once more.

Her favourite place – a tree trunk. A wide, massive branch that reached over the river, it cradled her body and, with a sigh, she settled on to the nuggety bark. Her favourite place. She'd be there for hours, wiggling on her back, looking at the leaves change colour, weekend after weekend, until they dropped off and the stark winter blue peered down; or else, straddling frontways, she'd gaze into the water, watching blossoms float by. And she'd dream; daydreams. Now, at last, she was here – at night! In the dark, in the shadows. By *herself*. She drank the cold of the night, breathed the chill air, turned on to the tree. And rested her cheek, and ear, on the silvery grey surface, listening to the tree's blood moving. She closed her eyes. Listened. To the tree, to the river trickle, to the sound of being free.

Whirr, whirr. No, whistle. Sound of air hissing through a gap in the front teeth. Milton. Close by, coming to her tree. Whero sat up, then relaxed. He was there, just in front of her, framed by a rustling stand of tall flax stems. Silently, he moved towards her. His jacket was unzipped, and the yellow flecks in his jersey glittered. He bent towards her, still whistling softly. One hand on her shoulder, pressing gently.

'Lie back.'

Whero wasn't sure what was going on, but she did as she was told. Leaned into her tree, feeling safe in her favourite place. Milton nuzzled at her neck, and was somehow planting something between her legs. It was his other hand, fumbling down there while he snorted in her ear. His bum was moving, slowly, softly, pushing against her. Whero squeaked, caught some of his hair in her mouth. Squeak. Then tried moving her own hips, pinned down by his weight. He stopped.

'Shuddup girl, don't move and then I'll finish.'

It felt funny. She was aching inside, and he kept pushing against her. His mouth was half open and his eyes were shut, and his bristles scraped her chin. It was beginning to feel wrong. She started to struggle, weakly, in a half-hearted way; then decided to concentrate instead on the dappled shadows that played across his face, and the tree bark, and the flax stalks moving, and the moon on her back too. If she shut her eyes, she could listen to the music of the water, running across pebbles and stones and clumps in the stream, avoiding that other place; she let her mind drift away with the water . . .

'Hey Milt! C'mere! Hurry up bro. I got it. I got the bugger. C'mon e-'

Yells and excited shouts a few yards away. Tuku bagging a big one.

'Hurry up e!'

Hands on his sister's trembling shoulders, Milton heaved himself up, turned, lifted his face, snorting. 'What, man? What the hell's the racket for?'

'Old Man Tuna. I got him. I got him.'

'What? Shit, you're having me on e' – in a split second, he was gone.

They were by the heaving, weed-choked water, Tuku hauling at the gaff, twisting his wrists, flat on his front, knees digging into the track, feet somewhere firmly in the green wall behind him. His older brother gripped the sugar bag, its flaccid mouth gaping and ready. They waited for the writhing and thrashing to die down; it seemed to go on forever. Whero looked on, not saying a word, wishing she was somewhere else, but staying still, being quiet. Wanting like hell to get away.

The tuna fought; tiring the two young men. It pulled, then stopped, then pulled again.

Suddenly it was loose. The gaff hung slack in Tuku's hand. Milton snarled. The girl sank far into the flax leaves, folded in their slick wetness, waxy hard.

Old Man Tuna had got away again.

Milton cursed his brother, and the fish. Tuku scrambled up,

brushed himself off. Feeling useless again; he'd never make a hero, an action man. But he'd always look good. And he liked to think. He really did. Angry, frustrated, they made their way back home.

'Hey, where's the girl?'

'E? Oh – I thought she was with you, e.'

'Nah. Musta gone back already, e.'

Slowly, murky sludge began to settle, blots of weed sitting damp upon its surface. Whero crept out of the flax, close to the river, eyes focused on the half-sunken log. Everything was still, quiet again. She thought of her brother, what he had done. It had happened, that was for sure. Yes it had. She remembered.

She couldn't take her eyes off the log, the bank of twigs and leaves and other stuff rotting in its forks. Night black, midnight black, something seemed to be waiting. She took a step forward.

A thick length of darkness arched out of the weeds, curled and twisted around, spun on itself like a great whip, sleek and shining. It skimmed across the water, it filled every part of that small, sluggish hole. Then it heaved once more, and was gone, plunging down into the mud.

Watching the Big Girls

She loved watching the Big Girls. Especially when they were in front of the mirror, in the toilets. They jiggled and jostled, and pulled each other around, and flounced and combed and fluffed their hair, and then suddenly they would go very very still. Looking.

Looking at each other, but most of all, looking at themselves. Wow.

And if a Big Girl came in by herself, that was even better. Tahuri would quietly shrink into a corner, making herself as tiny as possible. So small, that no one could hear her. But *she* could see *them*! It was exciting.

Her favourite Big Girl was Cassina. She should've been a boy, the old people said, named after Montecassino where her uncle was killed, long before she was born. Cassino. But that was a boy's name, they said. So here she was - Cassina, instead. And all the faraway, exotic, foreign, enchanting pictures that her name sounded to Tahuri were there - in her; in her eyes, and her hair, and her lips, and even her ears.

Cassina had beautiful ears, neatly tucked against the sides of her head, with finely rounded lobes. She wore stars on them; stars sometimes, and other times little gold circles that slept and slipped through the holes that Kuikui had drilled with a small hukere stick and muka thread. Ouch. She twirled them, her long Cutex scarlet nails bright in the gloss of her hair. Most of all, Tahuri liked the big gold circles - hoops they were. Gleaming and gilded, like the sun through smoke, or steam. But that was only on very special occasions; because the hoops were a secret that Cassina sneaked on when Kuikui and her mother, Karu, were not around. For some reason they didn't like the hoops at all, and they said so - but they never said why. They didn't like the fingernails, either; but made their stand on the hoops. This puzzled Tahuri, and made Cassina mad, but she wore them anyway. In sort of secret. Golden hoops and rich black curls that went all over the place, never ever sat in a decent beehive, but ballooned in fat black blossoms all over her head, and swirled around her shoulders.

Cassina was beautiful. She'd bat her long, dense eyelashes, and 'do' her dusky eyelids, and smile and sparkle at Tahuri, there in the corner by the rubbish tin. That was the neat thing about Cassina – she always noticed if her little cousin was there, and she always grinned at her, making Tahuri feel all warm and cosy inside.

Not like Trina. She was a witch, but somehow she had a lot of boyfriends with cars even; while Cassina got around with Heke, on his broken-down motorbike.

Trina was skinny, and white. Her legs and arms were the colour of the old old sheets at the pa – creamy-ish, and dotted. Sometimes freckles surfaced on her nose in summer, and she hated that, cadging a huge flax hat from Kuikui 'to preserve her complexion'. Whatever that meant. She'd come into the wharepaku, usually alone, her long neck swanning into a deep plum beehive, shades of purple in the reddish brown, spangled stiff with lacquer. Trina would turn her head this way, then that; lean towards the mirror and dig carefully at the clotted spikes that ringed her slanted hazel-green eyes, muttering about mascara; check the line of pink around her pearly little teeth; take a sleek powder compact from her clutch purse and cover the offending specks upon her nose; examine her eyelids too, and then, with a satisfied sigh, she'd stand back, and purr at herself. No ladders in the stockings. Good. Then, she'd turn once, twice, three times, on the balls of her white, slingback spike heels, and with a spring of stiff petticoats and frothing skirts, she was out the door. Without even a blink in Tahuri's eye.

Ben sometimes came in too, by herself. Bennie was special – she was different, and she was kind, too. Always had the Juicy Fruit or the PK chewing gum for little kids like Tahuri. She never looked quite right, though; her feet looked too big for her shoes, and her shoulders were as wide as Heke's. And her hair was cut funny, so it dropped like a dog's tail over her forehead, and went straight down to a vee at the back of her neck. Her clothes weren't very interesting either; really dry and colourless – purple shirt, black jerkin and grey pleated skirt, which hung half-way down her densely muscled, rocklike calves. Bennie – called Penupenu by Kui – had the legs all right. But she just used them to jump and dance and run around with; she never ever shaved them, like Trina; so very fine threads occasionally caught the light on her shins, because she hated stockings too. Along with all that dangly stuff that held them up. Tahuri decided that Bennie would've made a really handsome boy – she never wore make-up, but her eyebrows were jet black and moved from fat to thin above her dark dark eyes, framed in a lace of thick eyelashes. No need for the mascara there. Her nose was medium, and her teeth were big and white, and her smile was huge when she smiled; ear to ear, and dimples puckered up, and her sallow skin would glow.

Bennie'd be luscious too, like Cassina, if she really tried, thought Tahuri.

But Huhana was the one. She outshone them all, even Cassina. 'Suzie', they called her in Wellington; but when she came home, she was Huhana, Cassina's big sister, a woman of the world. While Cassina was tall, Huhana was short; and while Cassina was dark, Huhana was even darker: a ripe, rich colour like the polished oak piano the nuns had at school. Huhana wore fashions – her sister got the hoops from her – and when she came into the wharepaku, Tahuri gasped. Her eyes even popped. Wow. This was fashion.

Huhana had squeezed herself into a blood-red tight skirt that gripped her rounded hips, and slid in a silken line down her thighs. Her legs nipped together at the knee, making her full bum swing as she walked; and her ankles curved like bows from her black patent leather stilettoes. The same stuff, gleaming and brittle, encircled her waist, a tense band three inches wide, clipped together by a bright gilt buckle, set squarely beneath her blouse. Cut low, it was more of a bodice, with no shoulders or sleeves or anything like that. It was like a pari, without the straps – a stiff thing wrapped around the chest and back, covering the front, but showing a lot too. And Huhana was showing it for sure. The material was hard and black and grainy, and turned over into a little fold at her titties, which rose and jiggled and heaved like lush chocolate jellies. Tahuri's fingers twitched at the sight; they looked so soft, she was dying to touch them! Wow!

Huhana beamed at her; carefully looked herself over, powdering down the shine on her face. She'd unclipped the buttons on her slithery black gloves, and they were folded back over her forearms, so her fingernails, lips and skirt pulsed in the same hot colour.

Tahuri was enchanted: she watched as Huhana caressed the frosty glitter knotted at her throat, sparkling on her earlobes; as she slicked her smooth french roll, stretched and straightened her stocking seams, and pulled off her shoes and wiggled her toes, and put them on again, for fashion. And with a wink of silver eyeshadow and arched brows at Tahuri, she was gone.

'That was Suzie from Wellington,' the little girl murmured to herself.

Time passed, and Tahuri was still watching the Big Girls. And she was one herself, at last; but she couldn't primp and preen like the others – no way. Instead, she preferred to slouch, cool and silent, in the same corner, by the same rubbish tin, watching.

Reti reckoned she was a bit perverted, like her older sister Ben, who went away to Auckland and came back looking like Elvis. Tahuri thought that was okay, and went looking for Penu, but missing seeing her; she only stayed one night, then shot back to the big smoke, her royal blue lurex shirt flashing through the window of the bus. Her younger cousin snatched a quick look at the shirt, and waved and waved, promising herself to get one too.

A lurex shirt. Wow. Even better than the old black jersey she refused to take off, ever. Even at this creepy youth club dance, where all the big girls tittered while their parents and grandparents nodded, and the big boys flashed hungry eyes and razzed each other to ask a girl to jitterbug. And what came after the jitterbug?

Weddings and babies. Cassina with Heke and four little kids; Trina working in the draper's shop with a big puku, while her husband Lennie sold insurances, and Huhana now Mrs O'Shea in Dublin, with twins and an Irish sailorman. Bennie was the luckiest of all – she drove a dry cleaning van and grew more muscles, and didn't give a hoot about all that wedding stuff.

This made a lot of sense to Tahuri, so she stayed in the wharepaku, where none of the big boys could ask her to jitterbug.

She checked the toilet paper, and the washbasins, and the floors. She sat on the rubbish tin, and went out sometimes and got a drink, or had a dance with Reti, then back she came.

Always, when the Big Girls came parading by.

Watching the Big Girls. Loving them.

Sunday Drive

Aunt Jessie had the car for the afternoon, for the whole afternoon. She stood at the door, and rattled the keys in her sister's face. 'Are you coming?' she snapped, pretty eyes flashing with impatience and excitement. '*Please*, Pipiroa. It's not so much fun without you.'

The older woman paused, looked again at the ironing, a tangle of dull colours in the laundry basket, and the neatly folded pillowcases on the couch. 'Ae,' she murmured. 'Let's go then, we don't get the car every day. But Tahuri has to come, too.' 'That's all right.' Auntie Jessica beamed. 'It will be good for her to see all those flash houses.' 'To see how the other half lives, you mean,' Pipiroa snorted.

A few minutes later, freshened up and with small daughter in tow, Pipiroa closed the weatherbeaten door of her mother's house, her home. She noticed the peeling yellow paint and reddening hinges, crusted together like an old hakihaki, an old scab. She was looking forward to this outing; it was even better than the magazines, she knew that.

The old Prefect spluttered along, with Auntie Jessie's finely manicured fingers curled around the jiggling gearstick, her nails glossy bright with varnish. She was a nurse and natural polish was allowed, but red wasn't, she had informed her niece one day. Tahuri was fascinated – more women's secrets, the knowing of the Big Girls. She loved those long dainty hands, guiding them, as she sat up straight in the back seat, propped on two fat cushions, and peered through the window.

Clumps of bush lined the roadside to her right – the manuka scrub of Kuirau Park, patterned with pot-holed trails and tracks, silver-grey steam rising from great blubbing ponds of boiling water. Amongst a chunky ring of mossy rocks, the

Lobster Pool rippled greenly. Tahuri watched it go sliding by.

Soon they were heading into the posh part of town – just on the outskirts, nearing those streets where the flash houses were. Auntie Jess choked and clutched and jammed the ageing automobile into a lower gear, giggling in the soft autumn sunshine. She rolled the window down. Her sister did the same. So did her niece.

Together they looked out their windows. The two women murmured to each other in low, quiet voices, almost like a prayer. Almost as if they were scared the pakehas in their flash houses might hear them, and come out, and say something rude or unfriendly about them, about their car. Tahuri sensed it was something like that; but she listened to them talking like it was a list –

'Nice hedges.'
'Wrought iron fences.'
'Gates too. Look at that patio.'
'Lovely. What about the roughcast.'
'Yes and the red brick.'
'Oh! I *like* that rock garden!'
'Fernery, too, I'll bet. Out the back on the south side.'
'Probably. Lovely lawns. I love a lovely lawn.'
'Not with that slope, dear.'
'But a wishing well . . . Oh! those venetians are pink, Pipi!'
'Wii! They are too! And the French doors!'
'Mmmm, French doors. With a deer on the glass like frost.'

Slowly, they drove on, eyes shining with admiration. Huge gates. Concrete lions, sweeping drives scattered with crumpled leaves. Trellis roses. Big heavy trees. Ones shaped funny, too, like tops and boxes and triangles in a row. Skinny looking letterboxes, and big hefty ones with clips and clamps. And some homes with a wisp of steam from a pipe on the roof, tiled neatly. Not much roofing iron in this part of town. But still, the steam. Ngawha. 'They call it thermal here, dear,' wise Jessie informed her sister. 'Some of them even have what is known as a native bush,' she continued, pleased with her knowing so much. 'Full of Maori trees specially. What do you think of that?' 'Maori trees but no Maori people,' Pipiroa retorted; she was looking at a large, very new, pale pink brick house set back on a vast green lawn. Frothy white stuff like stiff petticoat material was gathered in the windows making scallops of curtains.

'That must be a Dutch house,' Auntie observed.

'I think I prefer venetians,' her sister said.

They had reached a dead end; they stopped. Auntie Jessie turned the key off. Gave it a rest. Dense greenery leaned across the road, threatened the puffing tired car. Huge old hedge of sticky dark spongy branches that Tahuri knew was full of walking-sticks. She was glad to be safe, in the back seat. She noticed her mother and aunt were leaning close together, and Auntie Jessie had her lacy white handkerchief out. She seemed to be sniffing. Tahuri busily looked out the window.

Amongst all the walking-stick hedge was a tall polished gate, with shiny bolts and studs. It was shut very tight, and was as high as a big man. The hedge went over the top of it, like an arch. Further along, there was another gap in all the woolly green growth. Tahuri couldn't see what was there, but the black gleaming front of a car poked out, just a little. She noticed a long, sleek, beautiful cat form, tiny and graceful, on top of the bonnet. Side on, it looked like Thomas the cat watching a bird, she thought. She heard her mother's voice. 'Jaguar. *He's* got a bloody Jaguar. That's why you brought us here.' There was anger beneath her words. And there was pain beneath Auntie's sniffles.

'When will you learn, Jessie girl? When will you ever bloody learn? This isn't for the likes of us, it's not. He's not for the likes of you. Him a doctor with his Jaguar car and lawyer wife and fancy bloody ideas. He's using you, using you. Can't you see that? And now us coming up here in this bomb, looking at the flash pakeha houses, you say. When will you ever bloody learn?'

Jessie sniffed and neatly tucked the hankie under the turned-over cuff of her cardigan. She started the car.

'I'm learning,' she muttered.

Rainy Day Afternoon

Something Tahuri learned when she was very young was how to make a sark. Her cousin Atea had come to stay for the holidays . . . She was big at twelve, tall and well-built, and the tip of Tahuri's head only just reached her ears. She was much bigger than Tahuri, with plump titties like cream buns that sat in a bright white bra with wide straps. Straps that Atea was always 'adjusting'.

'I'm adjusting my straps,' she'd grimace with a twisted mouth, as her fingers dug around somewhere on top of her shoulder, underneath her blouse. 'There.' And she'd smile, wonderful and warm and wide.

Tahuri had asked to see what a bra looked like on; she'd seen it off, and she'd seen Atea with nothing, but most of all, she wanted to see it on. Instead, she got a clip in the ear for being 'bloody dopey'. She couldn't figure that lot out at all. And the holidays were nearly over.

She was looking for Atea; she had finished all her jobs, and it was a rainy day afternoon, all right. Pouring down in buckets, the old lady said. Buckets and bathfuls of rain, tipped out of the sky by a mother fed up with washing by hand. The old lady always washed by hand, with Taniwha soap and the blue bag too. Those new machines were too dear, she said, and look what happened to Mickey-boy's arm with that wringer thing at Tia's. No. You couldn't trust 'em. Only strong arms did the job right. Strong arms of a strong woman. The old lady had strong arms, too.

Tahuri wandered into the back room and found Atea, who was busy ripping up thin thin still-snowy old old white sheets. The sound was sharp and swift, cotton tearing in neat straight lines. She clipped a few inches in, with scissors, then held each side firmly in each hand, and tore. The strips were about ten inches wide.

Without asking, Tahuri helped her cousin gather them up on the couch. When they started cutting them up into shorter lengths, she wondered what they were for. They looked too skinny to be nappies, but they felt the same. So she looked at Atea, opened her mouth.

'What are these for?' she asked.

'Sark,' came the blunt, strange reply. 'You know, for us . . . for us women when we have the rags on. Mate marama, you know about that. The rags on the barbed wire fence that the men don't go around when there's rags on it.'

'Oh,' twigged Tahuri, still not really clear. 'Oh. Them.'

'Ae, tena. That's it.' Atea bent her head, her pale hands skilfully folding, turning the sides of material in, testing the thickness, enjoying the soft feel of it, thinking how comfortable this batch would be. No lump sliding around down there, no chafing between the legs. 'It's for that time of month, you know.'

'Oh yes,' the younger one agreed, smiling away, soothing down her pile. 'I know.'

But she didn't really, and Atea knew that, too. Though she said nothing, just kept folding and feeling, showing Tahuri how to get them just right. Even if she didn't know what for. She showed her anyway, and soon the job was done. And the rain had stopped.

'Let's go have a look at the river, eh.'

The willow tree was too damp to sit on, and the long grass was wet and stuck to their legs, and the river still hadn't changed for all the rain, so they decided to return to the house. Empty. No one was home, except the cats, curled up snoozing on the arm chairs. Atea decided she'd go and have a lie-down; it was going to start raining any minute, and she felt like a nice rest.

They both went into the back room. All the sarks were stacked up into heaps along the couch, waiting to be put away. Opposite, the three-quarter bed with iron ends stood against the wall, under the window. A creamy lace curtain hung half-way across, blocking out the day in little patterns. Atea hitched it all the way down, making the room a little bit darker, and slipped out of her brown woollen skirt. She draped it over the bed end. She took off her cardigan too, and then slid under the bedspread, scrunching up her blouse. Tahuri looked away, but not before she had noticed how white Atea's legs were. Like the sarks, like the sheets. She felt her own skin, pale gold, darkening even more, as a blush crept slowly across her face. She was feeling funny. She roughly shoved the sarks aside, and plonked down on the couch. One stack tipped over, and Tahuri busily put it all back together again, while her cheeks got hotter.

'Come into bed, dopey,' Atea was propped up against the pillows, cosy and comfortable. 'You might as well lie down too, eh. There's only us home now. The old lady's probably gone off to see Auntie Jessie; she won't be back for ages. Tena, Huri. Piki mai.' She only spoke Maori when she was serious or really really sad. Most of the time she didn't, except when she was with the old people. Not many of the kids could understand her, and this made her wild, and when she got wild, watch out. Her grey eyes went like pins, sharp and cold and piercing. She really did look like a pakeha then, as much as she hated it; all pinched up and pink – a throwback, they said. To her great-grandfather, who was a Norwegian sea captain. With eyes like ice, chilly and faraway.

Tahuri coughed to make up for going red like that, and coughed again, not knowing what to say. She didn't want to say no, but she still felt a bit funny; and her feet were freezing from her holey socks and the walk down to the river. So she pulled off her dungarees and jersey and climbed in, snuggling close. Her toes twitched; the socks felt damp, too. She wormed them off, snuggled closer. She loved this – the warmth, and the soft smells, as she burrowed under the bedspread, and felt Atea's arm encircling her back, drawing her right in. They lay quietly together for the longest time, listening to the rain outside, not saying a word.

One of the cats walked in, tail in the air, sniffling. Sammy.

She jumped on to the couch, carefully leaned against the highest pile. Settled down to snooze again. Down came the sarks.

Both girls pretended they didn't see Sammy the cat. It was too warm to get out of bed and shoo her away, and too peaceful to yell at her. Or tidy up the mess.

Eventually, Atea breathed in a deep deep breath. 'Do you still want to see my bra?' she whispered.

Tahuri wriggled and muttered back, 'Ooh, yes.' She started feeling funny again. She was feeling funnier than ever, and she didn't know why. So she turned her face into her pillow, and heard the buttons on the blouse coming undone. Then Atea sat up straight, and stretched, moving her chest against her cousin's dark head.

'Huri mai,' she was talking from way down in her throat, deep.

'Huri mai, e, Huri.'

Tahuri just about choked. Blinking, she levered herself up. Her hands reached out. Then stopped. Then kept going. The bright white bra material felt stiff and unfriendly. She decided that she didn't like it. Straps and all.

'You look better without that on,' she judged. It was true. But she didn't know why.

Atea laughed. 'Then I'll take it off if you like,' she said.

Tahuri gulped. What was going to happen next?

Olympia

Whero had to go. She couldn't sit on the beach in her new purple jerkin suit and patent leather shoes. Besides, someone like Kuikui was sure to ask her to tell the story of the picture – they always did. She couldn't make it up – it was *Hercules Unchained*, and far too complicated. She'd just have to go by herself. Damn that Heeni, having to go back to Rotorua tonight, of all nights. After all their planning and sewing and polishing and fussing, getting ready to make a *scene*. It wouldn't be the same without Heeni, without her silly giggle and fluffy style. In fact, this whole thing had been her idea. Certainly not Whero's, who was usually a jeans, gumboots and jersey girl. None of this fancy stuff for her. But Heeni had insisted, and Kui had thought it was a good idea and shouted her the shoes, and Auntie Francie smiled that it'd be lovely to see Whero dressed up like a girl for a change. So they had all schemed away, and here she was, sitting on the concrete step going down to the beach, wishing for the moon to drop out of the sky, wishing for anything to happen. It didn't. Instead, Auntie Francie had bailed out the twinnies, and said that seeing as Heeni's not here, maybe Whero could take them along to the pictures, too. It was a shame to be so dressed up, and she could not go by herself, and the twinnies had been so good today and deserved a little outing. Oh God, thought Whero. No.

She knew that the twinnies would take off with their dopey little mates as soon as they got near to the place, and they'd sit in the front row and shriek and shout, and then they'd turn up at her side when it was time to go home. So she might as well have been on her own. They weren't much company – and she'd really stick out, looking like she did. But there was no other way – she had to go; she could not sneak back and put on her comfortable dear old clothes. She was stuck in this get-up, and that was that.

She heard the two little ones come down the path, faces flushed with excitement. Going to the pictures! With a twittering twin on either side, Whero strolled slowly along the pot-holed and patchy beach road. It was almost completely dark – just a faint streak of pale apricot tinged the deepening dark sky to the west, and the moon was climbing sturdily, half her face chewed away by shadow. The tide was in, noisily slurping along the rocks just below the footpath. A couple of cars passed; no one waved out though. They were pakehas. In front of Whero and her cousins, a large family group walked along purposefully, the kids all neatly rounded up and two-by-two; behind her, the voices of another lot carried through the crisp evening air.

They were almost there. Whero stopped. The twinnies started chattering about their mates. She gave them a bob each, and let them go. She stood there, by herself, scanning the scene.

There were four horses, a jeep and a big truck. Also the pakehas' cars, and three or four others, too. They gleamed eerily in the one chilling, bluish street light, that cast a strange paua haze across the gathering line of people. Tethered together at the rail by the general store, the horses shuffled and snuffled quietly, steamy breath rising from their soft nostrils. Altogether, they had brought fifteen people to the pictures. (A whole football team, thought Whero. Nah, that's wrong, half of them are girls! Anyway. That was hard work for the horses and they deserved their rest while they waited.)

Uncle Dave was sitting on his box with his money tin, his rich chuckling voice at full volume, as the younger girls slipped past him, blushing for their ninepenny tickets.

'What? Ninepence? It's ninepence for kids and one and three for you, 'cos you're a married woman and I know!'

No one argued with him, as he sorted out their ages; no one heard him say stuff like that to the boys. Never.

He got the line moving quickly – the twinnies had gone in already, but many of the adults hung around outside, and most

of them were men. Little pockets of fire flamed as roll-your-
owns were lit; the lilting busyness of talk, in Maori and English,
hummed above another sound. From one of the cars came the
melody of strong fingers dancing on steel strings. Whero
gulped. It was Mutu with his guitar. Oh shit, why did *they* have
to be there tonight? She saw other shapes shifting around the
car, leaning on it, moving about in the half darkness. About five
of them – Mutu and his mates, all working men now, with the
cash to flash and the style to show it. But they're still stuck here
at Maketu, Whero reminded herself. They're only farm
workers and they're only a coupla years older than me, and oh
shit, I wish Heeni was here. Or someone, anyone, oh God what
am I going to do? She peered at the shrinking crowd again,
seeking out a familiar, friendly, female face. There was no one.
They'd all gone in already. She was by herself. She'd just have
to go in by herself.

Just about everyone had filed in through the big corner doors
on the old building. 'Olympia', it proudly called itself in big
chiselled letters at the top of the front wall. Olympia! The
pakehas sniggered as they sat in their 'upstairs' seats, on a
platform fixed by beer crates; one hundred and sixty-four, and
all twenty inches high. What an upstairs.

Only the boys had to go in now, and Whero noticed that they
had noticed her.

She couldn't stand there a hundred yards away in the dark by
herself, she had to go in. She had to take the twinnies home, and
that was that. She gritted her teeth and walked forward.

The car door slammed, as Mutu got out. He was wearing a
jerkin too – it was black. So was his shirt. He stretched his long
arms languidly, looked at Whero, smiled at the boys. They lined
up along the car, leaning, shoulders back, hips out. She focused
her eyes on her shiny new shoes, on putting them calmly one in
front of the other, and managed to move past them.

It came like a smack in the face.

'Lookit her, all dressed up like that. Whakahihi. Anyone'd
think she was going to a blimming ball or something. Who does
she think she is, anyway?'

Biting her tongue, swallowing the acrid sourness of the lipstick, Whero lifted her lacquered head up high, walked to the door without a word, sniffed at an oddly silent Uncle Dave, and paid one and three.

Mirimiri

She felt like she weighed a ton, and she kept hearing Kuikui's voice, telling her she was getting too old for this stuff. Too old and too big. Too big, that was for sure. She shifted her right knee, wedged it along the other side of the tree's smooth trunk, balanced her bum on the very slightly swaying branch. If any of the old people saw her, that would be it. No excuses and no mercy. She'd get it for sure from Kuikui, who'd be the first to notice if even her little black rubber toe in its basketball boot slipped and dangled from the rimu tree's lush growth. Tahuri hoisted herself up further, into the branches. Bird's eye view, all right. She smiled to herself, brushed away the prickly tassel tickling her face. This was *worth* all the risk. And the shame, if she got caught. Or worse still, fell down.

Behind her, just beyond the corrugated red of Te Aomarama's roof, the wintry grey waters of the lake lapped and rolled. And below, all around, the marae was a mass of excited, milling, busy people, squashed together yet seething, like the steamy waters of the cooking ngawha, but with more colours than that, and everywhere a musty, familiar black. Raincoats and umbrellas, scarves and heavy skirts, thick socks, lace-up shoes, and heavy Black Watch tartan rugs. All excited, all looking in the same direction, up the road. On the wide pink concrete steps of Tamatekapua, near the bell, the koros sat in a neatly polished row, trouser legs creased sharp, and RSA badges winking even in the low bleak light of this overcast and chilly morning. Some talked to each other with smiles and scowls, one had his nose in a battered Best Bets, and another had his legs out straight in perfect line with his crustily carved tokotoko, his eyes shut while his lips seemed to be moving. A couple looked at the sky, firmed up their coat buttons. More just sat there, thinking about what they were going to say, who they were going to remember. And from his own chair, on big wheels like a pushbike, one koro held it over everyone, his rich, resonant voice bossing the women around, joking. They laughed back at him, tucking his woolly blanket snugly round his withered knees. They fussed about and were very busy, as if the rain, gathering above them, pressing down, just didn't seem to matter. And it didn't, really.

Tahuri moved her feet one more time. The black ripple soles of her boots gripped easily; she slid around, peered straight down. It was clear, almost completely clear. Soon, in maybe only a few minutes, the space would be just rows of empty forms; then they too would fill up, and the crowd be even tighter. Closer. She could hardly wait. Stretching her neck, she studied the entrance to the village. Most days it was just an ordinary street, lined with Maori Affairs weatherboard houses, dull green and cream and blue. Today, it was special. It was the gate into the village, the pathway to the marae, and little beads of steam delicately threaded into the air, telling the visitors that this marae, this village, were different.

She could hardly see them; they were bobbing around by their buses, packing themselves together, getting ready to come on. Then suddenly, quite suddenly, everything started to happen at once. And the ghosts began to move. While the softest, gentlest rain fell on their faces, the women's chant of karanga, of welcome, of mourning, of celebration, passed back and forth, then merged together, and the living and the dying and the dead were all as one. She sensed the weaving in the air around the tree, in the warmth rising from the ground, in the moving of the visitors, and the receiving of her own people, like they were all fitting together, fusing and fitting in to each other, slowly, easily. She switched off from the chant, and examined the oncoming ope, looking at them from the safety of her secret perch. And two faces — two figures — struck her, bolted right into her. She clutched the tree, rebalanced, concentrated on their faces. One, and then, the other.

The first was a middle-aged woman, wearing what looked like men's clothes. They had to be. Yet she was so strong, so confident — and so right. She looked great, and at first Tahuri couldn't take her eyes off her. There, second row from the front, just behind the chanting kuia. Compact and broad; the only man's hat amongst all the floppy ladies' felts and sober scarves. On a snazzy angle, and dark greyish brown, it was almost like the koros' — but more, well, up-to-date. Set just right, and though Tahuri couldn't be sure, the hair was really short too. Cut level with the turned-down collar of the big belted overcoat, hairy like a camel. Like the koros', but a much softer brown. Buttoned on the left side too, and the navy blue neck-scarf turned neatly in. 'Bet there's a shirt and tie underneath all that,' Tahuri said out loud to herself. 'I bet there is, and trousers, not sissy slacks. And the lace-up shoes . . .' The young girl was fascinated; it was all so right, so neat to see.

And then, right at the back, Tahuri noticed in the crowd coming on, a shining creamy-white guitar — and its carrier. Her face. The colour. The shape. The nose and the lips and the eyes. Most of all, the eyes.

The surging wave of visitors had paused; that chant gave way to snuffled weeping, the saddest sound of all; and then they fell back, as if blown by a silent wind, and the visitors' koros were sitting in the front, on the forms facing the huge carved house, while around them the visitors' kuia and other women settled down. Only a few people remained standing, the teenagers, some of the little kids, and most of the young boys. Tahuri looked at them all with interest, searching for that face. There she was, down there; Tahuri was transfixed again. She couldn't see that much, but the shoulders were mighty in the black peg jacket with big pockets. Funny-looking black pleated skirt, and that was all Tahuri could make out. The rest was behind the old Gibson guitar, half leaning, half carried against the young woman's body. Tahuri strained and stretched up in her hideout, wishing she could see those eyes again; the darked, roundest, biggest eyes she had ever seen.

As if she knew she was being watched, the visitor moved out of sight between two of the taller teenagers. Only the top of her head, wild glossy waves, shining and short, bright with the gems of freshly fallen rain, was visible. And bits of the guitar, spangled faintly with water.

Tahuri gave up for the moment, but determined to talk to her later. She changed position, looked straight down, wondering who was on the form propped up against the rimu. She peered. Neat! The big woman in the hat and coat, there at the very end! Her knees were bent apart, and she was leaning on them, her elbows on her thighs, her head forward, listening to the first whaikorero.

She was absorbed, concentrating. Her back was massive, pulling the heavy coat across; the scarf had loosened, flopping casually over her collar. Once she adjusted her hat, pulled at the rim, lowering it in front, and Tahuri gasped at the fine black gloves, old leather wrinkled to her hand's shape, snug. The big woman continued to sit forward; and against her, someone else was leaning thoughtfully, too. She was a lady dressed in dark navy blue, her suit jacket expensively cut in three panels fitted on her narrow back. Flung across her shoulders, and pinned to one with a gold-rimmed oval of greenstone, was a thin shawl, night colours blending with the jacket, and on her head the daintiest hat. Over her knees was a rich mohair rug. She kept leaning against the big woman, snuggled. She must be cold, Tahuri thought. And still the big woman continued to watch the welcoming orator, to take in every word. He was winding down; he finished with a dramatic flourish, and a piercing female voice began an ancient song. The showering rain had stopped. Below her, the big woman leaned back.

She turned to the smaller one next to her. The lady looked around, jostled just a little, and was still. Her hands, pale and fragile, long fingers like the petals of pikiarero, were on her lap, twining and twisting thin fabric gloves. She wore no rings. She trembled and shivered in the cold. And in a flash, it happened. The big woman had taken her gloves off. Tahuri caught the gleam of gold links pushed through the cuff, turned back to reveal a man's watch. Frozen stiff with fascination, she gawked.

The big woman reached for the pale shivering hands, covered

them with her own squareness, brownness. Covered them
briefly, then slipped her forefinger and thumb around the
small one's wrist, made a dark bronze ring, a playful bracelet of
warmth. First on one, then the other, which she grasped,
sliding her hands along the chilled flesh, caressing, lightly
fondling, tracing the smoothly perfumed palm with calloused
tips. Tenderly. Then she took one fragile hand, and with swift
grace, touched it to her lips, pressed it to her face, returned it to
the rug. So sudden, and so very very subtle.

No longer shivering, the lightly patterned shawl cuddled up
against the thick brown coat. Their side - the visitors' first
speaker - was on his feet, opening his responding speech with
an echoing song poem. The big woman leaned forward, elbows
on her knees. And again, she listened.

They were staying down the pa; Tahuri found out from her
Auntie Tui as they sweated over the lunch dishes. Some were
going out to Whaka, but the buses that came in that morning
were going to sleep at Tamatekapua. If this wet weather didn't
clear up, it was going to be one hell of a weekend; the haka
groups would be performing inside the Ritz Hall instead of
outside at the Soundshell, and a full house was guaranteed.
Already the dining-room was overflowing, they'd had four
sittings for lunch, and this was just the first lot of buses. Auntie
Tui worried a lot, and no wonder. Tahuri moved across to the
knives and forks and risked stabbing herself horribly; she
jiggled them around in their tins while her younger cousins
grizzled and snapped their tea-towels. With a bored sigh, she
tipped the cutlery out, and set to drying it, cutting herself off
from the clatter and chatter around her in the huge communal
kitchen. She daydreamed about the big woman and the little
one, and she wondered how she could get to talk to the teenage
girl with the guitar. It was too early to go over to the meeting
house - more buses were arriving, and more manuhiri were
coming on, so they wouldn't start moving inside until all the
welcomes and speeches were over. So now it was dishes and

setting tables and doing the kai and hanging around helping out until then. Sighing, she got on with it.

Auntie Tui was shouting at her through the din. About getting the extra pillowcases from her shed, taking them inside now that the paepae had cleared for afternoon tea. This was her chance! She'd have to find the extra pillowcases first – there weren't that many, she could carry them herself – then she'd be free, in Tamatekapua and around the house, where she could look for those visitors, admiring one from a distance – and maybe getting to know the other.

The shed was a small wooden shack behind Auntie Tui and Uncle Jack's house which faced on to the marae. It was old, really old, and they reckoned it was probably one of the first pakeha-style places built in the pa. Layers and layers of paint marking years of time chipped into the weatherboards – blue, apricot-orange, lime green, blue again, then dark green, and finally, Maori Affairs cream, which Tahuri would peel away at the corners, with an old pipi shell or pocketknife or whatever was at hand. She liked discovering the old colours – but even more, she liked going into the shed: it smelled old, and lavendery and interesting; of freshly washed and ironed linen, and mothballs; of kapok mattresses piled in a corner with pillows packed ceiling-tight on top, of firmly rolled whariki standing up in another, of kete full of pingao blades hanging yellow from the ceiling, of bundles of kiekie, of cut, scraped flax, of things ready for weaving. And against one wall, all the way along, there were shelves covered in wallpaper, nailed down flat, with cartons full of sheets, and two big washing baskets heaped with pillowcases. And on the lowest shelf, in a cedar glory box, the special linen, for special visitors.

This time, the shed was almost empty of its stored treasures. The whariki were covering the meeting house floor, every single one, and all the sheets were out. So were the kapoks, but three worn-out feather mattresses made a bouncey-looking bed just under the window, bundled together, puffed up and plump beneath a heavily patched sheet.

Tahuri quickly set about her job. The afternoon light was fading fast, and she wanted to do more than find the extra pillowcases. There they were, two dozen crisply cleaned and pressed, in the washing basket. She checked to see who was outside the door – no one – then had a sneaky look into the glory box; this temptation was always too much for her. The lid flipped open on its golden cords; the gentle scent of cedar drifted out; usually packed tight, it was less than half full because of the special visitors. But at the bottom, a few wonderful pieces lay flat, and Tahuri picked them up, one by one, letting them delicately unfold, spilling out their colours, and their patterns, and their rare, incredible beauty. They were like the pictures in library books and calendars, like the pictures pinned up in the art room at school. Except these were real, and they were made in the pa by all the old kuias, and they were wonderful. Much more than pillowcases, these. Embroidered and elegant – roses starting rich red on the inside and getting lighter and pinker as the petals moved from the middle, with bright leaves and thorny green-brown stems that twined around each other, making curves and corners; a spray of golden kowhai, threading shades of yellow and brown, with tiny emerald leaflets linked together. These two sets were too worn to be put out any more, so they stayed in the box. With the oldest pair of all, the set that Tahuri liked best. Respectfully, caringly, she lifted one high above her head, framing it in the mottled window. She gripped the fuzzy, fraying edges – and smiled at the design. Worked into the aged material was a carved face, splendidly shining eyes, with wide mouth and poking tongue, the cheeks curving outward and upward, meeting cleverly together, forming a circle of chainstitch, the colour of fading wine. Auntie Tui had confided that this set was a bit peculiar – the old people were very particular about who she put them out for, and they were really very old, the oldest in the cedar chest. So now, they were hardly ever used; and each year, each hui, the special visiting kuia and koro they were meant for were fading just like them; passing away, or ageing, becoming too frail and too old to go out any more. But when Tahuri looked at that design, she felt warmed and strengthened by the pattern, and all the faces that had ever rested on those pillows smiled back at her, sad, and happy, too. Pleased that she'd seen them, and more pleased that no one had caught her, she lovingly stroked their thin, silky lines, and folded them back into well creased rectangles to be placed again inside the glory box. She took one more deep breath of cedar, stung this time with mothballs, and gathering the extra pillowcases under her arm, she set out. Evening was falling.

The girl was under the rimu tree, sitting on the damp form, tuning her guitar. Everyone else was in, or around, the dining-room, and Tahuri had just finished stuffing pillows. Her nose was full of kapok and sneezes and feathers, and she needed to stay outside for a while. Here was her big chance. She walked over and sat down, trying to be cool. Hoping not to sneeze.

'Kia ora.' Big cheesy smile. Charming. 'You had some kai?'

'Mmm. Ae. Yes thanks.' Continued to fiddle with guitar keys. Short fingernails, and tapered fingers. Callouses.

'Oh. That's good.' Smile not quite so cheesy, but still cool. 'Um. You settled in okay then?'

'Ae. Got me a nice warm bed next to my auntie, eh.' Turned to look at Tahuri, hands still. Grinned from ear to ear. 'This place is really neat, eh! Spooky, though, all the steam and boiling water and stuff, but I like it. You live here?'

Tahuri couldn't believe it. Heaven! It was so easy. She smiled the big cheesy one again, and was extra charming, extra cool.

'Ooh yeah, this is my home ground, my place. D'you want to have a look around? I'm a real good guide, know all the sights, where to go in the dark even!' She swallowed the last phrase. Her new friend looked at her, stood up - wow, she was big - slung the guitar over her hefty shoulder, gestured at it.

'I'd better take this inside first,' she said. 'Then - let's go! Oh yeah - my name's Mirimiri. Mills for short.' She laughed.

Tahuri laughed too; it was almost as if this manuhiri was the one in charge here; but no way, this was her place. She grinned back. 'I'm Tahuri,' she replied. 'Nothing for short. Eh, Mills, welcome to Ohinemutu, centre of the universe.'

Together they crossed the marae, and went into the big whare.

Mills had said their group was on at a quarter to nine. That meant Tahuri had to get to the Ritz by half past eight, so she had to break out from the kitchen by eight. It wasn't raining as hard, and she looked forward to the long walk across town — if she could shake off the little kids. The clock said twenty past seven.

After what seemed another lifetime of dirty damn dishes in the dining-room kitchen, she asked Auntie Tui if she could go. The answer was 'Sure, wait for Uncle Jack and he'll take you and the kids.' Tahuri knew what that meant. She thanked her auntie, said she felt like walking, and was off out the door.

Masses and masses of people; smells of raincoats and damp Brylcreme and wet blankets and sharp perfume and roll-your-own cigarette smoke, all crushing around the doors, pushing to get in to the concert, out of the rain. Being not all that big, Tahuri squeezed through the side, popped out into another throng of big heaving bodies. She pretended she was looking for some important koro, and made her way along the wall, skipping from person to person, getting a kiss here and a pat there from relations dotted in the end seats or standing along the way. Close to the stage, she found the perfect spot; huge bunches of flax flower stalks and thick green blades were pushed into a sawn-down forty-gallon drum, edged with coloured paper and filled with sand. She wedged her bum on to it, taking care to keep the arrangement just right. She let out a long, happy breath, and waited, looking at the stage.

They came on. What an entrance! The crowd went crazy, yelling and stomping their feet and whistling enough to make your ears crack. It was fantastic! Two sets of performers, coming from both sides of the stage at the same time; voices strong and fabulous, their harmonies so rich and soaring, their karanga shrill, penetrating beyond the rowdy audience, lifting their greetings proud and high to the old people gathered in the crowd. And then the ranks joined together, and they were into their first action song, and everyone sitting down below went even more berserk, clapping and laughing and bellowing, and through it all, Tahuri heard the guitar.

The big woman was in the front row; their whole line-up was large and majestic, but she most of all. And her hair was very short, even mannish, and her teeth shone, and her hands quivered and her eyes flashed, and she became the song. Her stance was upright and muscular, but, like the others on either side of her, there was a softness too, in her firm large arms and bulging shoulders and rounded hips; there was laughter, there was grace. Piupiu superbly cut, a fanning arc of black and white, densely plaited, each strand fingernail fine, belted into taniko at the waist, swirling out to make its own music, to reveal ankles finely chiselled, and shapely, swelling calves. Even dressed up like all the other women, she was exactly right.

Tahuri tried to spot Mirimiri. At the side, on the guitar, fingers moving, arms flexing, keeping pace. She was in full costume too, with something else; a short cloak trimmed with hukahuka, the black tassels shimmering as she strummed. On her head, clipped down but out of control, her taniko headband wobbled around uncomfortably, as if the elaborate red, white and black diamonds and triangles just weren't meant to be there. That, Tahuri considered, didn't matter all that much. The group was fantastic, just fantastic and she just couldn't wait to tell her new friend.

They didn't see each other again until the next day, Sunday, at lunchtime. Tahuri had got caught at the Ritz by Uncle Jack and one of those nosey little kids, so she had to go home with them; she was still too young to be walking the streets that late at night on her own, the family said. So home she went, with the magic of the concert lighting up her heart. And the rain started falling hard, again.

The manuhiri were leaving after lunch; boxes of food were being packed to take on the buses, and some had already left that morning, early. Mills had come into the kitchen to help; Tahuri was beaming. They worked away, cutting up scone bread, buttering it, the younger girl raving on and on about the fantastic entrance. And action song. And haka. And poi. And of course they had won the competitions. Mirimiri just smiled away to herself, muttering thank you, and kept on with her job. Tahuri went quiet, thinking about the bus leaving soon, and how they'd not had any time together at all. It made her feel sad, and also a bit frustrated. She chopped away at the scone. Around them, the other women were busily cutting paper, stacking the bread, slicing the meat, wrapping the kai, and packing it up. Through the window, sheets of rain lashed across the marae, and thick clouds of steam rose rolling from the ngawha, blocking out the view.

Auntie Tui came in, looking as if she had something important to say. She stood up straight, though she was very short and round, and dramatically wiped her hands on her apron. This was her sign for everyone to pay attention; the women stopped working, and looked at her attentively.

'Well, girls,' she declared in a very loud voice. 'There have been major slips on the road out of town, the roads are all blocked up because of the rain. They're clearing it out, but the last buses won't be leaving until tomorrow lunchtime at the earliest. So! That's it!' Sighs and smiles from everyone; concern for the visitors and their families waiting for them at home; with murmurs of softer conversation, the women slipped back into the familiar routine. The boxes would have to be unpacked; more meat would have to be put on; someone would go for the milk. Auntie Tui went into action; everything was moving again.

Tahuri wanted to jump and shriek for joy. She looked across the bench at Mirimiri; they both stopped working. Something clattered to the floor. The butterknife. Swiftly, the older girl bent to pick it up; it had fallen by Tahuri's foot. She paused for not even a minute; softly, quickly, she linked her fingers into the top of Tahuri's boot, pressed her knuckles against the skin, pulled down the sock. Dug in with her fingernails, then hoisted herself up, staring directly into the other's wide gaping eyes. Challenging.

'Neat.' Mirimiri was smiling. 'That's really neat! Eh, Ta – who knows what the night will bring?'

Tahuri gulped. That spot on her ankle was electric, burning with excitement. Oh yes. Neat, all right. And she knew just the place, too. For the night to bring something.

Auntie Tui agreed Tahuri could sleep in the shed that night – if she moved the mattresses back in, the ones they weren't using any more, and packed the place up nice. She was glad, too; Uncle Jack had gone off with her key ring with the shed key on it, and she wasn't sure when he'd come back, and she didn't want the place open all night long. There might be drunks wandering around, looking for a warm place to sleep it off before they went home to face Mum.

'As long as you have a mate, lovey,' her eyes twinkled. 'Not a boy, mind you.' Not likely, her niece flashed in her head. Yuk.

'Ooh no Auntie, never. I'll tell Kui, then I'll ask Mirimiri – you know, their guitarist, eh.' Auntie Tui nodded, her head full of all the jobs she had to do, and walked off to do them. The old people had decided to make the most of so many people in the pa for another night – some of the koros were going to the club with the workers for a few spots, but most of the oldies and the young ones were going to stay on in the whare kai, have a bit of a social and some items, and maybe play cards later on. The home crowd was also gearing up to entertain, though they'd do their items in ordinary clothes, not dress up in concert gear. Tahuri was looking forward to it – she enjoyed the haka, knew she was useless at the poi, but would get up anyway and have a go. She was feeling a little bit funny, knowing she'd be up there in front of Mills – but fair enough, she'd seen her friend on stage the night before.

The bathhouse backed on to the lake; it was made up of rocks and mossy concrete and slippery old timber fencing that kept the pakeha tourists out during the day. Half of it was roofed over with tin sheets, but the pool itself gleamed under the clouds, the night, the stars. It was almost round, with one side squared off, and steps forming sunken seating just below the water level. As with most of the older baths in the village, sandy natural springs bubbled up from the bottom, and a narrow drain channelled the overflow down into the lake. Tahuri was too shy to light the candle in the corner – baths like this never had electric light. Massive clouds lolled across the moon, the steam rose like fat ballooning sails, and every now and then, the stars would twinkle through. Ha. It was enough that she and Mills were there, alone, together. Without saying anything, they undressed, hopped quickly in, not looking at each other. Water closed over them soothing, like a caress. They hardly talked at all – they were both tired out by the long day and running around between showers of rain, heaving mattresses back into the shed, stacking them up for Auntie Tui. She'd had them on the go all afternoon, and by night time they were stuffed. After the concert, they had both sneaked outside. Tahuri suggested they go for a bath, while everyone else was still in the dining-room. And off they went.

Mirimiri wasn't used to the mineral water, so they didn't sit in there for very long. They didn't touch much either – just kept thoughtfully apart, pulling on their clothes, tying their towels around their hips. Hands brushed very briefly as they passed through the door, stepped out into the swirling steam.

Some of the boys were sitting on the form under the rimu tree. They were talking and smoking and trying to be tough. One of them stood up. Hands deep down inside his crotch, he sauntered towards the young women.

'Gotta match, Ta?'
'E hoa, you know I don't smoke, eh.' She kept her voice very even.
'Huh. Oh well. That's all right. You got some fire for me then, girl?' He moved towards her, pelvis first, cocky.
'No, I bloody haven't, you smartarse. Piss off or I'll tell Uncle Jack on you.' Her face was flaming. The boy laughed gruffly, swaggered around. He was getting the results he wanted. He wasn't too sure about the big dark one, though. She looked as if she was winding herself up for a scrap. And she was as big as him, maybe even bigger. She seemed to be sizing him up. Huh. He didn't care. The boys were there.
'You piss off, Miss Whakahihi Too Big For Her Boots. Don'wanchoo anyway. You're not what I call a real woman.' Guffaws and harsh laughter from the other boys. 'And as for your mate – haw haw haw. All a man can see is –' He stepped back into the safety of the pack, standing restless. 'All a man can see is your teeth . . . Moonshine.' Chortling with the strength of their numbers, their maleness, they blundered off, kicking at rocks on the road.
'Stupid little prick, I could've bitten his fucken head off, he'd get teeth all right,' Mirimiri swore, fists clenched hard. 'I could've wasted that little black shit. They make me sick. I can't stand the stupid bastards.' They watched the boys disappear towards town.
'Me too.' Tahuri scuffed along, embarrassed, humiliated. She was used to them razzing her, but she still hated it. And them. They thought she was pretty because she was short and had long straight hair and a fair complexion. But Mills was sort of the opposite, nothing half caste about her. Oh damn those creeps for spoiling the evening, damn them. She started talking to blot out her bad feelings.
'Do they really make you sick?' she asked. The older girl looked away, paused for a minute.
'Yep. In more ways than one. Let's say I'll put up with them and that's about it. I can't be bothered, you know. Can't figure out what it is about them that's meant to make us go silly – boy

crazy, you know. Matetane! What!' she giggled to herself; it sounded rather strange. 'Anyway, darl. What about you?'

Tahuri started going red again, but fired ahead.

'Well. They make me sick, too. I don't like them much at all. And besides I think I'd sooner go with girls, if you know what I mean!'

She blurted the last bit out quickly, remembering how those fingers in her boot had cut her up with pleasure. Quickly, just in case Mills hadn't meant for it to be like that. The answer came back, soft and clear.

'Hey, that's neat. Me too.'

But they kept on walking apart. Tahuri started up again. She was excited, and there was something she wanted to know.

'You know that big woman – your auntie – the one wearing the man's hat. Is she like that?'

'Well. Ah. We're not supposed to talk about it outside the family – you know what I mean. Ah. Ah. She could be. But it's not for me to say anything, eh . . .' She trailed off. That subject was more or less finished. The younger girl went ahead and bounced on to a new one. They were close to the shed.

'I like your uniform,' she chattered on. 'Especially yours, with the little korowai and stuff. Did you have to make all the gear yourselves?'

'Yeah. Oh, my sisters helped me with mine, and all I had to do was put my name on everything, permanent like. And Auntie – the big one, you know, she gave me that dumb headband. I labelled that, too. Dumb. My hair's too thick and it's too short and I hate that headband. Can't seem to stick it on straight and it always comes off because I hate tight rings around my head squeezing out my brains and I wish I could lose the bloody thing!'

Tahuri recalled how funny and awkward it had looked; she touched Mirimiri's arm, cautiously, on the shirt sleeve. The skin underneath felt warm, and promising.

'I reckon you'd look good in anything,' she whispered.

They were at the shed. Mills had said earlier that she'd sleep there too, help Tahuri keep the drunks out. Tahuri, whose blood was pounding, whose gut was creaking like the door. The two young women linked little fingers, and went inside. Bolted the shed shut. And wordlessly, curiously, hungrily, they fell into each other's arms.

Mirimiri had been in too much of a hurry to dry herself properly. Her skin was clammy from the bath; the faded black flannel shirt stuck to her in patches, she wanted to peel it off. Not yet. She pushed herself against Tahuri's body, they sank down on to the feather mattresses, cushioned and moulded, nesting their own hollows. Legs entwined, towels a sodden knot on the floor, dropped instantly the door had locked. Tahuri's jersey prickled at her neck and throat; the wool was damp and itchy, she didn't know whether to take it off or leave it on. So she left it on, and her underpants too, though they were soaking wet and not just from the bath. Mills leaned into her, hands found their own way up her jersey, dragging it off, bunching it at her armpits. She hauled it over her head; the other girl's came off too.

They looked at each other. Sat back, slightly away from each other, and they gazed and gaped, at the ways they were so different, and yet so much the same. Mills was big; football shoulders and strong neck, and dusky shadows in her throat, dipping in to full breasts that sat up high and round, and jiggled slightly when she moved her arms. One was draped across her chest, covering its points, the elbow resting on her puku, a hard bed of muscle. Her other arm was up behind her head, supporting it on the squash of feathers. Tahuri noticed a hairless scoop of armpit, silken and completely bare. She instantly felt shy about her own hairs sprouting away up there – not that she had many, but all of her family and most of her girlfriend cousins had none at all, and she was the only one with them, like a pakeha, and it made her feel funny and different, but maybe with Mills that didn't matter. She hoped so. Still, she kept her arms down, and covered her front, too. God, they were so flat she looked like a bloody boy – sometimes that was cool, but tonight she wasn't so sure, admiring Mills' big ones – and oh shit she was so *white*. Almost as white as the sheet, she realized with horror, as her foot found its way towards Mills, whose deep brown toes flexed and unflexed lazily. Like the paws of a huge black cat. Then Mills moved. She dropped her hands, kneeled forward across the piled bedding, and grabbed her, pulling her down.

Their bodies fitted together. Their mouths met, softly moist and flowering open, licking and leafing delicately; their fingers found their own way, probing, circling, kneading. Tracing the satin liquid smoothness of skin, teasing out the scatty scales of ticklishness, measuring the lines of magic-making pleasure. They hung on, and kissed and smooched and kissed.

Their underpants were tight and damp and tangled, a barrier. And the heat grew there, a strong, lustrous aching that seeped through the straining cotton, and tangled in their pubic curls. They throbbed and gasped and thrust into each other. Thighs scissored together, Mills' largeness overwhelming, she folded Tahuri right in to herself, they rocked around laughing between long heavy smooches, tumbling to the floor, as the feathers flattened. Tahuri was galvanized, moving herself up, moving into the other one's body, feeling her bone down there somehow sinking in to all that softness, feeling something else, too, pushing on her. Hard, it was, Mills' hip bone or front bone or whatever it was, it didn't matter, pushing and grinding and pushing her over the cliff, over the cliff; but she hung on to the edge, she hung on, tight. Following Mills. Catching up. Or waiting for her.

Hands on her breasts, lips, too. Four breasts. All the same, all different. Small firm mounds, raspberry nipples, tiny dimpled rings, teeth rimming them, sinking in to the skin, or heavy ripe plum-purple swellings, juicy and eagerly plucked, their secret creases luscious, underneath and in between ... The samenesses and the differences; supple fingers spun and stroked, gently spidering their way about a shuddering surface of curves and flatness, bunched flesh, and taut skin. Pulsing; earlobes nipped and nuzzled, purring; and every bone along each back lovingly studied and stroked, with hands bold and calm and sure, counting, claiming. Going in, going home.

She groaned, her body arched and bucking gently, a melody of rippling muscles tingling all along her side, beneath her puku, along her flanks. Her eyes were shut, squeezed, her mouth so wide, swallowing the dark, and she clutched the hand, rolled on it, rolled over it, replaced it with her own, removed her own, let it find its way in to the other's place. For more, for more. Taking, giving, taking again. The underpants were beginning to be a bit of a damn nuisance.

'You know what?' They paused, cheekbone leaning against cheekbone, eyelashes almost woven together, breath mingling. Through the shed window, the moon sailed high, ringed with the eerie, haunting colours of more rain. Clouds wobbled across her face.

'I reckon we should take our underpants off.'

The next day started far too early for both of them. Auntie Tui had them up and helping with breakfast, then it was cutting and buttering more bread like they did the day before, for the boxes to go on the bus. They worked amidst the fuss of clearing up, stacking away, folding down, and generally getting ready to go. Tahuri and Mirimiri were quiet around each other, but staunch. They both knew that was probably going to be it, unless they saw each other at the next hui, and Mills wasn't very sure about that because she was thinking of going down south with her brother-in-law's shearing gang. But she'd try and get there; there was always someone coming up this way. And there was the holidays, too.

Too soon, it was time to go. Mills had the guitar under her arm again. She was leaning against the bus, and Tahuri was examining the rubble around her feet, tugging at the waistband of her jeans, or pulling restlessly at her plait. Just about everyone else had climbed aboard. The two young women looked at each other; the dark one knew that she mustn't be the last one to get on the bus. She set her guitar up against the wheel, shoved her hands into her jacket pockets, half grinned at Tahuri, who smiled back. They embraced, hugged each other tight for as long as it was all right. They didn't cry. Just held each other, Mills' quick knowing hand sliding into Tahuri's back pocket, for the briefest second. She kissed her near the corner of her mouth, just missing it, and she whispered secretly, tenderly,

'Ka kite, darl. I mean it. We'll do it again, eh. Honest.' She grabbed the guitar, and was up the steps and out of sight.

Tahuri stood there, staring. She hated goodbyes, hated them. 'Ka kite, Mirimiri. Have a safe trip home. See you next year, eh? See you again!' I hope I hope I hope I hope I hope I hope, she muttered fiercely to herself as she turned her back on the bus and rushed back to the whare kai. There was heaps of work to do.

Before going in, she stopped at the rimu tree. The plank seat was still there. She sat down, trying to pull herself together, to stop the tears, to remember all the night's soft sweetness. Something dug into the left cheek of her bum – a hump in the back pocket. She pulled it out.

Black red white triangles and diamonds, patiki and nihotaniwha, the loveliness of a taniko headband shone in the dull winter sun. It was lined, too, neatly sewn in black cotton. And the name, boldly, beautifully embroidered in elaborate silk capitals. Chainstitched, in bright wine. MIRIMIRI. She squashed it hard against her nose, and breathed in deep. She wiped her tears on it, too, for they were coming now.

And with a bursting heart, she set off for the dining-room.

Red Jersey

Whero limped back to the bathhouse, her back sore, and between her legs aching from where they'd kicked her. She was sore all over, even at the very ends of her body, her toes bruised from kicking too, and her fingernails split and chipped and purpled, groaning as she pulled the twisted rubber band from her hair. Clotted with small nuggets of stickyness that'd be interesting to peel off when the pain died down. Her head boiled noisily, the brain almost breaking through her skull. She couldn't – wouldn't – move it; watery sounds like ocean waves rushed through her ears; hot, raging hot, like the ngawha down in the back yard.

She twined the unravelling dark red wool in her hand, and leaned against the wall. She would be all right. She had to be. For Kuia's sake.

Damn those bitches for snagging her jersey.

It was her birthday present from Kuia. Damn them. Tenderly, careful with herself, she began to take off her clothes. Lucky the bath was in. She sank into the healing water.

She'd been beaten up. By those two half-caste cunts. And their dumbo pakeha mate. God, it hurt. And it just wasn't fair – it wasn't her fault, it wasn't. It was Heeni's. Not hers. But Heeni had gone back to Horohoro and left Whero looking like a drip. Like a mug. And what the hell for.

She was still trying to figure it out when Teresa Taylor had grabbed her and pulled her behind the bus at the Travel Centre car park. Glass bracelets tinkling, her nails a slash of scarlet, digging into Whero's arm.

'Gotcha, you queer cunt!'
Wham! Slap! Boot!
'Take that you black bitch! In the cunt!'
Thwack! Bang!

Whero curled up tight, all hard, cut off like she did when her stepfather was on her.

But these were girls. From school. The Taylor sisters. She'd have to give them a go.

So she rolled to the side, back against the rough concrete wall; puha and dandelion tickled her neck. Breathed in deep, let them keep hitting.

'Yah! Fucken yellow bitch can't fight back! Fucken queer!'

Boof! Whack! Kick!

Knees bent right up under her chin, wet with saliva and tears and snot and panic. Knees bent up. Focused on the big one's legs. Shot them straight out, and Teresa Taylor was on her pretty pink arse, stiff petticoats like candyfloss ballooning over her; left wrist sliced and bleeding as the bangles from the Hindu shop splintered on the asphalt.

Whero was on her feet, at the sister, Camilla; whose mouth was half open and gulping at her tough, gorgeous Teresa wailing and winded in a pile of starched and blood-speckled tulle. Gulping like a fish.

Slam! Pow! The fish mouth collected a hard little fist as Whero let her have it. No time to think. Just fight back and get the hell out of it. She dodged and Teresa's leg whipped out and Whero was down again. Taking Camilla with her as she fell. Punching at her face, whacking her. No mercy. This was to the death.

Fat white fingers were pulling at her hair, ripping at her jersey, spitting, clawing at her as she tumbled around, with Camilla not letting go. Sue. Where the hell did she come from? Sue. She was dirty. She'd propped Teresa against the bus door, then barrelled in to get Whero. She walloped and kicked and scratched and dug – she rammed her hand into Whero's mouth, missing her eyes, and howled as the teeth came down. She seethed and sprayed and Teresa, recovered now, came in to pull the mad Maori queer off her sister. And do her.

'Hey! What the hell are you girls doing there?'

Pommy bus driver, with his little tin box and navy blue uniform and peaked cap with a badge.

'What's going on?'
They froze.
'Gonna get choo later, queer.'
Helped by Sue's large strength, Camilla staggered up. Then the three were off.

And Whero slowly creaked herself up to half standing, half slouching on the wall. She tried to stay straight, and muttered painfully through the red, 'It's nothing, it's nothing. Nothing's going on . . .'
She wobbled towards the street.
The bus driver fumbled for his keys. Damn coloureds, he thought out loud to himself. Young girls too. Thought I'd left all that in Birmingham.

Most of the mess was washed away, but Whero couldn't touch her hair. Not yet, too sore. The clumps throbbed away, teasing her. She rested her neck on the edge of the bath, concrete and cracked, where little furrows of green moss sucked in the steam. She stretched her legs and arched her arms, and thought about that Teresa Taylor. And then she knew. She knew why Teresa was so wild. But it still wasn't fair.

The Taylor sisters had come from Auckland. Their mother was small and dark and scared-looking and never ever went to the pa or anything; and their father was this big brawny pakeha with a red face and rusty whiskers. His eyes were a funny colour when they weren't scrunched up like a pig's – green and glittery, like the swift summer currents of the river. Teresa's eyes were sort of the same; but pretty. Like her bracelets. Which is why Whero noticed her. And smiled at her across the hall at assembly, and wanted to be friends.

The other one, Camilla, was different. She was a bit darker – dark enough for it to matter, but not as dark as Whero. Which was why, she supposed, Camilla quickly started to hang around with that slob Sue, who had a swimming pool in her back yard. Ha. Whero had one, too. And not just one – five of them, if you counted the ngawha by the river. But for Camilla, it looked important to have pakeha friends in their new school; so she did.

Teresa, meanwhile, didn't seem to need friends – she was contained; she hardly even saw Whero. Who was too black to bother with, anyway. Probably.

But Whero was struck by Teresa Taylor, and plotted to get to meet her. She found an ally in her cousin, Heeni, who was in Teresa's class in the daytime and Whero's bed in the night-time. At least, during the week – Heeni stayed during the week to go to school; she was two years older than Whero and was already looking for a job. She knew about life; and she knew how to take pleasure from it. Part of this was getting Whero to give her love bites as they snuggled into the feather down mattress of the big old bed. The love bites often went on to something else too that Whero especially liked doing, that Heeni told her to shut up about. As long as she had her love bites to skite over at school – from some luscious mystery man no one ever met or knew – Heeni was happy. And Whero was really happy too.

Then along came Taha, fresh back from Malaya, and ready for some action on the home front. He lived next door, and soon Heeni was sneaking over to his bach in the middle of the night. Taha was cool and sophisticated and had a real hi-fi. Whero felt left out, just a kid. Resentful. Heeni felt guilty as hell. No more love bites and the rest for her – no more of that sorta stuff she always felt a bit funny about afterwards. What could she do with her little cuzzie-mate? Like a convenient gift, Teresa Taylor turned up on the scene. And Whero was gawking at her.

Heeni talked to Teresa one day as they changed periods. Told her about this cousin who was real interested in meeting her. Never mentioned it was a girl. Intrigued, Teresa looked slowly over Heeni. Noted her flawless golden skin and laughing dark eyes and wild red wavy hair and bright white toothpaste smile. Really fine-looking. Really Maori-looking. Secretly, Teresa liked that. So tall too. And quite slim. If the cousin was anything like her . . .

Teresa Taylor perked up. She needed a distraction from this boring new school and smelly little town where the Maoris still lived in their pas, and the pakehas were all snooty, except for the oversized Sue. Maybe she'd meet this cousin after school. It was something to do.

Tuesday, half past four. That would give her time to go home and get changed, do herself up. And check this Whero out. Whero. Red. Nice name for a Maori boy who might just look like Heeni; she couldn't wait to tell Camilla and Sue. And take them along too – just in case he was a creep; then she could laugh in his face and prance off with the girls. She had nothing to lose.

Whero was excited! She was meeting Teresa Taylor at the Travel Centre at half past four. Maybe they'd go and have a milkshake and Whero could ask her about life in the Big Smoke. She wished Heeni could come – she was so nervous – but Taha had taken her home to Horohoro for the night. So she was on her own.

Heeni had told Teresa that Whero would be wearing a dark red jersey and black stovepipe pants. Whero knew what Teresa looked like.

Half past four. At the Travel Centre. She waited. And she watched the clock. And waited, eyes scanning the street, for the places Teresa might come from.

Quarter to five. She shrugged her large shoulders in the warm new wonderful jersey, and slicked the creases on her stovepipe pants. Maybe Heeni was having her on.

Just then, the hand grabbed her.

MAORI WORDS USED IN THE TEXT

I have used Arawa tribal dialect. In some instances, Maori words have been rendered plural by adding 's'. This is an English-speaking practice, and is frowned upon by people who use Maori as an everyday mother tongue. However, I've written the language as it occurs in many bilingual communities today.

e: pronounced as in 'ten'. Interrogative, or a way of finishing a comment.
haka: traditional posture dance, with chant
hakihaki: scab, sore
hapuka: groper, a bulging-eyed fish; *polyprion oxygeneios*
harakeke: flax; *phormium tenax*
hautonga: southerly wind
hoohaa: pron. 'haw-hah' fed up, bored, impatient
hui: gathering, meeting, occasion
Hui Topu: huge festive gathering organized by the Anglican Church
hukahuka: thrums or tassels of muka on korowai
hukere: also manuka, a tree; *leptospermum scoparium*
kaati: enough, sufficient
kai: food, to eat, eating
ka kite: farewell, lit. 'Be seeing you'.
kapai: good, fine, okay
karanga: chant of welcome and of mourning, cast only by women in rituals of encounter or crisis
kare: dear, sweetie
keha: shortened form of pakeha, usually abusive
kehua: ghost
kete: woven fibre bag or basket
kia ora: greetings, hello; lit. 'Let there be life'.
kiekie: a climbing plant; *freycinetia banksii*

koro: elderly man, grandfather
korowai: finely dressed flax cloak with hukahuka
koura: freshwater crayfish; *paranephros planifrons*
kowhai: a tree; *sophora tetraptera*
kuia: elderly woman, grandmother
kuku: mussel; *mytilus canaliculus*
manuhiri: visitor
manuka: also hukere, a tree; *leptospermum scoparium*
marae: open space in front of whare whakairo
mate marama: lit. 'moon sickness', menstruation
mate tane: lit. 'man sickness', promiscuous
moko: tattoo, usually seen on the chin of kuia
mokopuna: grandchild, grandchildren
muka: fibre of harakeke
ngawha: boiling spring, thermal
ngeru: cat
nihotaniwha: triangular weaving pattern, lit. 'dragon teeth'
ope: crowd of people, usually manuhiri
pa: fortified village; in more recent times, village or settlement
paepae: bench or seat for orators; ritual threshold
pakeha: caucasian, white person
pari: stiff woven bodice, part of costume
patiki: diamond weaving pattern, based on the flounder fish;
    rhombosolea plebia
paua: abalone shell with blue/green iridescence inside; *haliotis*
piki arero: native clematis, lit. 'climbing tongues'; *clematis paniculata*
pingao: sand dune plant; *demoschoenus spiralis*
piupiu: thrummed skirt made of harakeke
poi: ball on string, manipulated in dance
puha: edible sow thistle; *sonchus oleraceus*
puku: tummy, abdomen
raupo: bulrushes; *typha aegustisolia*
repo: swamp
Ruapeka: a small warm water lagoon in Ohinemutu
taiaha: traditional striking and thrusting weapon
Tamatekapua: elaborately carved meeting house in Ohinemutu

taniko: traditional weaving technique and form
Te Aomarama: Anglican Church hall in Ohinemutu
tika: correct, proper
tokotoko: walking stick, staff
waiariki: lit. 'chiefly waters'; mineral pools
waipuke: flood
whaikorero: oration, speech, oratory
whakahihi: snobbish, conceited, vain
whare: house, dwelling
wharekai: dining hall
wharepaku: ablution block, toilet
whare whakairo: carved meeting house
whariki: woven fibre floor mat

PAKEHA WORDS USED IN THE TEXT

Some expressions I have used are slang or colloquial English of 1950s and 60s New Zealand.

A and P Show: Agricultural and Pastoral Show
a bob: a shilling, old NZ currency, worth about ten cents
AFFCO: Auckland Farmers Freezing Co-op (acronym)
bach: small house or cottage
changed periods: moved from one class period to another during the school day
chooks: chickens; also chookies; domestic fowl
cords: corduroy trousers
kit: bag, basket; from Maori, kete
lav: toilet, lavatory
one and three: one shilling and threepence, worth about 15 cents
roll-your-own: handrolled cigarette
sarks: sanitary napkin
shearing gang: working team of sheep shearers
skivvie: longsleeved sweater of light fabric
swandri: heavy woollen shirt favoured by farmers and outdoor workers, hunters and fishers.